"Well, now, Margaret, seems to me I got somethin' special to keep in my memory out of it. I can live with people teasin' me."

Tony leaned in to kiss her.

"Could you live with it for a few more months?" she asked before their lips touched.

He pulled back, met her gaze. "Meaning?"

"Last night when I said I knew who you were, that you owned the ranch, you said your ranch owns you. Am I remembering that right?"

"You are."

Maggie drew a deep breath. "Okay. So, then, I have a proposition for you."

The last one had resulted in their being naked together. If this one involved that again, he'd be saying yes faster than a bronc bursts out of a chute.

"I'm listenin', darlin'."

"Marry me."

Dear Reader,

This novel marks my 25th for Harlequin/Silhouette Books—and my first-ever cowboy hero. Because I knew nothing about cattle ranches, I began to research them. I found a wonderful site online for the M Diamond Ranch in Rimrock, Arizona. I sent them a note. Would they be willing to answer questions about cattle ranching in Arizona for me?

A most enthusiastic yes came back to me. Laurance and Peggy Ingham own the ranch, and Larry became my mentor. E-mails flew back and forth, then finally a note that said, "Why don't you come down and visit us? See what it's really like?"

I had the best time! They plunked me on a horse for a trail ride, put me up at their own home, treated me to a cowboy cookout of rib eyes and cowboy beans and all the other fixings. There, wrangler Kevin Kennedy explained what being a cowboy really meant. And I took away with me an appreciation for the land, for the history and for what Larry and Peggy are trying to do, which is to provide a sustainable existence for all who live on the ranch (people, livestock and wildlife). The cowboy traditions need to be kept alive.

If you're ever in the area, take a trail ride with them and see the beauty of the land for yourself. The experience changed me forever.

Susan Crosby

THE RANCHER'S SURPRISE MARRIAGE

SUSAN CROSBY

SPECIAL EDITION®

Published by Silhouette Books

America's Publisher of Contemporary Romance

Special thanks and acknowledgment to Susan Crosby for
her contribution to the BACK IN BUSINESS miniseries.

 SILHOUETTE BOOKS

ISBN-13: 978-0-373-24922-0
ISBN-10:   0-373-24922-5

THE RANCHER'S SURPRISE MARRIAGE

SUSAN CROSBY

believes in the value of setting goals, but also in the magic of making wishes, which often do come true—as long as she works hard enough. Along life's journey she's done a lot of the usual things—married, had children, attended college a little later than the average coed and earned a B.A. in English. Then she dove off the deep end into a full-time writing career, a wish come true.

Susan enjoys writing about people who take a chance on love, sometimes against all odds. She loves warm, strong heroes and good-hearted, self-reliant heroines, and will always believe in happily ever after.

More can be learned about her at www.susancrosby.com.

For Larry and Peggy Ingham, and Kevin
and Stephanie Kennedy—generous, selfless, inspired
and industrious people who know what's important in life
and go about achieving it. I admire you all so much.

Chapter One

Maggie McShane blamed her lifelong weakness for cowboys on John Wayne movie marathons, a New Year's Day family tradition. Those happy childhood memories pierced Maggie as she watched a cowboy mosey onto her Arizona movie set. He rivaled the Duke in looks, from his thick brown hair and blue eyes to his looming height. She felt caught in his crosshairs, the way his gaze zeroed in on her, and it was everything she could do to turn away from him, and prepare for her next take outside a rustic old barn on a working cattle ranch.

"Take your mark, please, Maggie," the director said.

"Quiet on the set!"

The take was a different angle of an earlier shot, a sweeping arc that would end on a close-up of her face. Her expression was supposed to convey determination, but also a little insecurity.

"Cut! Let's do it again. A little more grit this time, Maggie."

"Right." Maggie wondered who the cowboy was. Why was he on the set? Who gave him—

"Cut! Where's your head, Maggie?" the director, Mac Iverson, asked.

Startled, she met his gaze, seeing more than curiosity there. Maggie was always prepared, always on cue. Darn cowboy. "Sorry, Mac."

"All right. Once more. Action!"

The cowboy stuck his hat back on his head, covering that beautiful hair that curled down his neck a little…

"Cut!" Mac came up to her. "Do you need a break or water or something?"

"It's the heat," she said, lying, embarrassed at not being her usual professional self. "This time. I promise."

After two more takes, Mac said, "Good job, thanks." Noise and activity picked up again. They were winding down for the day. Only two shots left, neither requiring her presence.

Leesa Post, Maggie's longtime personal assistant, approached, her ever-present notebook in hand. "Looks like we're getting out of here early tonight, Mags. What do you want to do about dinner?"

"Room service, but first a long, hot shower. I've got dust in every pore."

"Arizona in September. Pretty dry stuff."

"I'm learning that." Maggie lowered her voice. "Who's the cowboy talking to Mac?"

"I dunno. Want me to find out?"

Did she? He'd already brought back too many memories—and distracted her in other ways, too. Not a good thing. And yet, she wanted to know. "If you can, discreetly."

Leesa cocked her head and grinned. "You're an engaged woman."

Maggie rubbed her left ring finger, but the diamond-and-platinum engagement band Scott Gibson had given her three weeks ago was in her bodyguard's pocket for safekeeping. "I'm not looking for a date, Leesa. I'm just curious. Mac doesn't allow many strangers onto his set."

"Probably a money guy. I'll be right back."

Leesa was the queen of efficiency. She'd been an extra on a TV sitcom Maggie had starred in as a child. They'd become fast friends at the age of six, twenty-five years ago. When Maggie had needed a full-time assistant, Leesa jumped on the bandwagon, deciding she hated being on that side of the camera, and wanted a shot at helping take care of Maggie's skyrocketing career.

"His name is Tony Young. He owns this ranch," Leesa announced quietly when she returned, holding up her tablet as if taking notes from Maggie.

"Is he as tall as he seems?"

"Ninety-five percent of the world's adult population can see the top of my head. Everyone is tall to me."

"Yeah, I've been meaning to tell you it's time to get your roots done."

"Ha, ha. Mac says you can go—7:00 a.m. call tomorrow. I've got your pages, and Dino's getting the car."

Maggie would have to walk past Tony Young, ranch owner, the Duke personified, to get to her trailer to change into street clothes. Manners dictated that she stop and introduce herself, but there was something about him, even from this distance, that made her hesitate. Definitely the John Wayne connection, she decided, therefore the emotional link to her parents and their time spent watching old

Westerns. Even though they had died a long time ago, the loss was still raw sometimes. It was the reason she'd waited so long to do a Western. She'd thought she was finally ready for it. Maybe she was wrong.

"Hey, Maggie," one of the cameraman said, coming up to her. "A few of us are headed to the Red Rock Saloon, outside of Sedona. We checked it out a couple of nights ago. Wanna come?"

"Thanks, Pete, but I'm wiped out. Another time, though, okay?"

"You got it."

She started to head to her trailer, then turned around. "Is it a real cowboy bar?"

"It's nothin' fancy, that's for sure. Got pool tables, though." He grinned, knowing how much she loved to play the game.

"Then you'd better save some of your hard-earned cash for when I do come." She waved and walked away, noting that the cowboy had left during the exchange. So. The decision was taken out of her hands. He was gone. She hadn't even heard his voice to know if he sounded like John Wayne, too.

Silly thought…

In the car a half hour later, Leesa said to Maggie, "You want a laugh?"

"Always."

Leesa placed a copy of *Meteor* in Maggie's lap. The gossip weekly's cover photo had Maggie resting her hand on her abdomen and a wistful expression on her face. "'Twins on board? The real reason for Maggie and Scott's quick wedding.'"

Knowing Leesa expected her to smile, Maggie did, but something twisted inside her, too. Twins. She should be so lucky. She craved a family. After being orphaned at ten, she'd been raised by her maternal grandparents, the paternal set having died before she was born. Now her beloved Gram and Gramp who'd raised her were gone, too. She knew she shouldn't complain—after all, a lot of people loved her—but she wanted someone who was...*hers*. Scott would be that, then before too long, children, she hoped. Family. Stability. She would prove it could be done successfully in Hollywood.

"So, seven weeks now constitutes a quick wedding?" Maggie asked, handing the magazine back to Leesa.

"For you. In the public's minds, anyway. Your fans would've expected a long engagement from you, and a ceremony to rival royalty."

"Which is pretty much what's happening, isn't it? I've been promised it'll be the wedding of the year." Even though she would've preferred a small ceremony with her closest friends, she'd agreed to a big, elegant, star-studded event as a favor to an old friend, Jenny Warren, who'd convinced her to hold the wedding at a brand-new hotel, The Taka San Francisco. More important, Jenny was counting on Maggie, and Maggie never let her friends down. Regret had dogged Maggie ever since she'd said yes. She should've trusted her instincts and done the intimate, surprise wedding. Now it was too late. She couldn't let down Jenny and her family. They were counting on the publicity.

Even more important, Scott had admitted to wanting the big splashy affair, too. And Maggie wanted to make him happy.

Maggie's car pulled into the Desert Canyon Resort and Spa parking lot a while later. She followed her bodyguard/driver, Dino, as they climbed to her room on the upper level. He'd been with her as long as Leesa. Sometimes Maggie had to keep a team of bodyguards with her, but the production company had private security on set, and she was keeping a low profile in Sedona, not in need of an entourage, hotel security doing extra duty there, too.

"You've been quiet, even for you," Maggie said to Dino as she toyed with her engagement ring. He'd handed it to her as she'd climbed into the car.

"Yep," Dino said, hands clasped, legs spread and planted, staring straight ahead after he unlocked the room door and stepped aside.

A few seconds passed. "You, too, actually," she said to Leesa. "For *you*."

Leesa grinned. "Yep."

Maggie pointed a finger at her. "You've got a secret. You're both in on it."

Dino and Leesa exchanged looks then said, "Yep," just as Maggie opened the door directly into the living room of the elegant suite. A tall, blond man rose from the sofa. Blond? She almost didn't recognize Scott, her fiancé of three weeks. His hair had been dark brown two weeks ago. On the other hand, she'd been blond instead of her current auburn. Such was the nature of film roles.

Funny—her heart didn't skip a beat at seeing him. But she put that thought from her mind, telling herself she was very glad he'd come, and wondering why she was trying to convince herself this should be so.

"We'll leave you two lovebirds alone," Leesa said. "Let me know if you need anything. Have fun." She winked at Maggie, then she and Dino headed to their adjoining private suites.

"Well." Maggie hurried toward Scott, smiling. "No

warning? No fanfare? Just you?" When he didn't answer, she wondered if she'd said something wrong, and she tried to laugh it off.

"This is a wonderful surprise, Scott, although I think it means our publicists are falling down on the job. Usually events like these are orchestrated for maximum press. Which reminds me, did you see the latest issue of *Meteor?* Apparently I'm pregnant with twins, which is why we're getting married so quickly." She laughed again, then put her arms around him. When he didn't hug her in return, she leaned back, realizing that not only had he not smiled at her yet, but he hadn't even spoken a word. "What's going on? Why aren't you on location?"

"It's a quick trip, just for tonight. Maggie…"

She didn't like how he said her name. She let her arms fall to her sides. "Should I be sitting down?" she asked.

After a moment he took her hand and led her to the sofa. His head bent, he ran his thumb over her diamond.

Her stomach churned as realization hit her. "You're breaking our engagement," she said, pulling free.

He nodded.

Maggie swallowed around the hot lump forming in her throat. *Abandoned. Again.* "Another woman?"

"Yeah. I'm sorry."

"Someone I know? Someone you're working with on the movie?"

He rubbed his face with his hands. "You'll find out soon enough. Gennifer Bodine."

Gennifer? She stared at him, speechless, until she gathered her senses. "Are you crazy? The woman sleeps with all her leading men. And then some."

"Rumors."

"Oh, maybe she skipped Charles Jansek. He's seventy-two, after all." Then it hit her. "You've slept with her already."

He finally met her gaze. "I'm in love with her. I'm really sorry, Maggie."

She shoved herself up and walked across the room. Tears burned her eyes and throat. Not now, she thought, pressing her fingers to her eyes. She'd known all along that their "romance" was one-sided. She just hadn't wanted to admit it. And he wasn't worth tears…

Calm down. Just calm down. Think this through.

She stood at the picture window staring at the glorious view of the red rocks of Sedona, feeling…feeling what? She wasn't sure. A mix of confusion, hurt and…relief? How could she feel relief?

"So, how do you want to handle things?" Scott asked. "I'll take all the heat, of course, but do you want the announcement to come from your team or mine?"

Maggie made herself focus on the situation. The breakup had to be dealt with carefully in the press. She would have time for her emotions to surface later, to figure out how she felt and how she would deal with it. She'd gotten way too good at keeping her feelings at bay.

"I have to think about it," she said. "And talk to my agent and my manager. And Garnet. Can't make a move without my publicist's input, right? You know the drill." Anger began to take center stage, but she didn't want to give him the satisfaction of seeing her reaction. "What I need at the moment is for you to keep it to yourself for a while so that I can figure out the next step."

He crossed his arms. "Two days, Maggie. That's plenty of time. I want to move forward."

"Go public, you mean." Just as he had three weeks ago

when they'd announced their engagement to the world. He'd been in a hurry to make *their* relationship public then, too. "I'll be in touch. You can go now."

"I'm really sor—"

"Just get out."

He got to the door, put his hand on the knob.

"Wait." She yanked off her engagement ring and tossed it. He caught it on the fly. "I've heard Gennifer doesn't mind secondhand goods."

He looked at her with the puppy-dog gaze that made women everywhere swoon. "Someday you'll be glad about this."

"That would ease your conscience, wouldn't it?" She watched the door close then latched it behind him. She didn't want any more surprises.

No wonder she'd barely heard from him. His movies, all hard-driving, nonstop action, took longer and were more physically exhausting than hers, so she'd believed him when he said he hadn't had any free time.

What a joke.

They'd had a *deal*. A commitment.

Maggie clenched her fists. Her jaw hurt. She couldn't stay in the hotel, couldn't spend the evening as if it was like every other evening. Her gaze landed on the envelope with the script pages she was supposed to learn for tomorrow.

"Later," she muttered. She wouldn't sleep tonight, anyway. She headed to the shower, tried to wash off Scott's betrayal along with the ranch dirt.

The ranch. She turned off the water, reached for a towel. The cowboy. The cowboy bar.

That's what she could do. She could meet the crew at the Red Rock Saloon.

But how to get herself there? She didn't want Dino to drive her. He was way too good at reading her, so she needed to stay away from him, at least for tonight. She wanted to just hang out with the crew, figure out how to announce her broken engagement. For tonight, anyway, she could fake that life was still okay, or else she didn't have the right to call herself an actor.

Maggie phoned the concierge, generally the most discreet employee in the hotel. After a short discussion, she'd lined up transportation. Then she called Leesa and Dino and told them she didn't want to be disturbed under any circumstances until 6:00 a.m. Dino grunted assent. Leesa gave her the verbal equivalent of a wink.

Maggie dressed in her favorite jeans and boots, added a new red Western shirt bought for the trip, stuffed her ID and some bills in her pocket and sneaked out of the room. She felt better wearing the outfit. Stronger, more in control. The boots gave her confidence, too, as if her father was walking beside her. He'd instilled in her his love for John Wayne and the cowboy ideal of standing tall. If her father were here he'd be reminding her she'd survived a whole lot worse than her fiancé falling in love with someone else.

She left her hair down so that it could fall against her face, hiding her as much as possible. The concierge met her in the parking lot, handed over the keys to his own car and gave her directions to the Red Rock Saloon.

She was bound to be recognized, no matter where she went, but she hoped for enough time to anesthetize her pain a little first.

Maggie counted eight vehicles in the saloon parking lot: six pickups, one van and a motorcycle. She parked her borrowed, ridiculously out-of-place Ford Focus next to the van she figured belonged to the film crew.

Deciding to get the lay of the land first, she stepped over an evening's worth of cigarette butts on the ground and eased open the back door, wincing as it creaked. She slipped inside. The jukebox played a twangy ballad. Pool balls clacked. Low, male voices drifted down the dark-paneled, rough-hewn hallway, then the higher pitch of a woman's laugh. The scent of beer filled the air. The bar probably served little else.

It was her kind of place, a statement that would surprise a whole lot of people. She may have grown up in front of the camera, but behind the scenes she'd been raised simply. She felt ten times more comfortable in a bar like this than a fancy restaurant or trendy club. And tonight, when she was hurting, the whole place seemed to wrap her in a hug.

Maggie peered into the main room. She counted thirteen people, including the bartender. Four were from her crew, all crowded around the pool table. Only two were women, both in their twenties. The other patrons hung out in small groups, either at the long bar or around tables.

Absurd disappointment struck her. She'd hoped the cowboy would be there. Why would he? Should he be able to read her mind? Catch her wish drifting through the air that she wanted to see him, the memories he evoked both comforting and exciting? Crazy. It was absolutely crazy to be thinking like that.

She walked to the pool table, dug into her pocket and pulled out a ten-dollar bill, which she plunked down by a corner pocket. "I'll take the winner," she said, getting the attention of the players, cameraman Pete and grip Warren.

"Hey," Pete said, grinning. "Thought you were tired."

"Got my second wind."

"Grab yourself a cold one. Warren here's gonna be done in a minute."

She wandered over to the bar. "I'll have a glass of what's on tap," she said.

The sixty-something, ponytailed bartender nodded and grabbed an ice-cold mug.

She put a fifty-dollar bill on the counter. "That's for me and those four over by the pool table. Let me know when you need more, okay?"

He eyed her. "Okay."

"Aw, Mags. You don't hafta do that," Pete called out.

"You'll be paying for it one way or another," she said in return. "I'll just be using your winnings."

Hoots and hollers came from her friends. She grinned. She leaned against the bar and took a sip. As she lowered her mug she saw a photograph of herself on the wall, among a slew of other star photos, male and female. She moved closer to look at them. A few were autographed to a guy named Tex. Most weren't signed at all.

A black-and-white drew her closer. It was her cowboy in full rodeo gear, his signature scrawled across one corner. The shot looked to be maybe twenty years old.

"Are you Tex?" she asked the bartender.

"Sure am."

"These people all been through here?"

"Most. Some are just particular favorites of mine or my regulars."

Which meant she was a particular favorite. She took another long sip, happy to be honored at the Red Rock Saloon, then started toward the pool table.

"Miss?" Tex said, gesturing with his head to come closer.

Maybe he didn't recognize her. After all, she was platinum-blond in the picture and wearing a gold sequined dress—the Oscars ceremony from a few years back, when she was a presenter.

"I'd be honored if you'd sign your photograph before you leave," Tex said. "And in case you're wondering, if anyone here bothers you, I'll send 'em on their way."

She appreciated his concern. "I'd be happy to sign the picture for you. I'd be happier still to send you a new one from this film, in my ranch gear."

"That'd be mighty kind of you."

She smiled then took herself over to the pool table to let her natural competitiveness dispatch her erstwhile fiancé from her mind for a little while longer.

Pete handed her a cue stick then lifted the rack away, indicating she should make the break. She chalked the tip and took her position.

The back door creaked open. Boot steps echoed on the wood floor, strong and steady, but she ignored them, concentrating on her shot.

"Hey, champ," Tex called out. "Been a while. What brings you out this way?"

"Just wonderin' what the wind blew in," the newcomer said.

"Want your usual?" Tex asked.

"You remember my usual?"

Maggie aimed, made her shot, scattered the balls. One dropped into a pocket. Oh, yeah, this felt good. Focus, shoot, play. Forget.

It was just what the get-over-him doctor ordered.

Chapter Two

Mug in hand, Tony Young walked over to a corner table where he could watch the whole room, not just the star attraction, Maggie McShane. She was so focused on the game she was playing, she hadn't noticed him come in, hadn't looked his way once, which he found interesting. He would've thought she'd be aware of everyone in a public place like this.

She was a good-looking woman, even prettier without all that movie makeup. Seemed to him she hadn't bothered with any tonight, like maybe people wouldn't recognize her with a clean-scrubbed face. Hell, he'd known it was her the moment he'd come into the room, without even seeing her face. The woman had a body on her that— Well, it was *fine*. Why she'd always been billed as the girl-next-door type made him scratch his head. She played those roles, sure, but didn't anyone factor in her body?

Images of red satin sheets came to his mind right away, not country-blue denim.

America's Sweetheart, people always pegged her. It was kinda sad they couldn't be more clever.

He wondered how she felt about the nickname. Was curious, too, about how big her ego was.

He watched her line up her next shot, leaning over the pool table, giving him a nice full-on view of her rear, all tight and round in her second-skin jeans. She was friendly with the guys, but not overly, and they were respectful of her, for all that she was wiping the floor with them at pool.

Tony kept an eye on the other patrons, too. He didn't know any of them, as he wasn't a regular anymore. What drinking he did was usually at home, with trusted friends. His hard-drinking days had ended with his rodeo career. He didn't miss either of them much.

The music on the jukebox stopped. He was thinking about choosing some songs when the two other women in the place went over and plunked some quarters in the machine. One of them gave him the eye, smiling a little. Hell, she was young enough to be his…well, his little sister, anyway. He was forty, and she probably hadn't been legal for long. He looked away, then something made him look back. She was focusing on Maggie McShane with her cell phone camera.

Tony let his chair drop to all fours. He shoved himself up and moved into her line of vision, then kept going forward, hitching a thumb toward Tex to take care of the woman. Tony kept walking until he came up behind Maggie, still blocking the view.

Maggie straightened slowly. He didn't move. Although he wasn't quite touching her, he was close enough to feel heat, so he knew she could, too.

"Move back," she said calmly.

Her friends descended on him. He stopped them with a look, then waited for Maggie to turn around and face him, which she finally did, blushing slightly when she met his gaze.

"Unless you want a photograph of your pretty little behind spreading like wildfire around the Internet, you'll stay right here with me until Tex deals with that amateur paparazzi over by the jukebox. She got a good bead on you when you were chuggin' your beer, America's Sweetheart," he said, continuing to be her personal barricade from photo ops. "And maybe you could call off your posse, too, since I'm just tryin' to help."

"It's you," she whispered. "John Wayne."

"No," he said slowly, wondering about her sanity. "The name's Tony Young."

"Oh, I—I know. I asked…"

She'd asked? About *him?* When? Why?

"You own the ranch."

"Well, technically, it owns me," he said, then was bumped from behind by one of her friends.

"Look, cowboy, you need to give her space. Now."

He did. Not because the guy said to, but because he could see Tex escorting the picture taker and her friend out of the bar. Two men followed, swearing the whole way, but whether it was at Tex or the women, Tony didn't know. Maggie peeked around him, watching the scene.

Heat. She was all fire and heat. On top of that, up close she was stunning, all bright blue eyes and dark, rich hair and soft, full lips—and freckles, pale and scattered across her nose and cheeks.

"She's used to having her picture taken wherever she goes," her friend said.

"I don't doubt that." He didn't take his eyes off her, and she was staring right back.

"I appreciate your running interference, Mr. Young," she said.

"Tony." Her head reached his chin. It was rare for a woman to match him so well in height. "Where's your entourage?"

"I ditched them. I…needed to get out. Had something to think over." She leaned around him again and said to her friends, "I've taken enough of your hard-earned dollars tonight."

Tony noticed her smile didn't reach her eyes. He also noticed she wasn't wearing her engagement ring. Woman like that should be sporting a rock that would blind you. "You know the two-step?" he asked her.

Her brows arched high. "Actually I just learned it for the movie. Big scene at a barn dance. Why?"

He tossed his hat onto a nearby table and held out a hand in invitation. "Let's see if you had a good teacher."

It took her a few seconds but she finally stepped into his arms, where she fit perfectly. Tony liked the two-step. It was one of those dances where the closer you got, the better you did together. Man leads, woman follows. Simple. Could be a sexy dance, depending, but didn't have to be. Given the heat flowing from both of them, though, he figured it was going to knock sexy into the next territory.

He was right. The heat was combustible as he drew her a little closer every so often, until he could feel her breasts touch his chest. He heard her suck in a breath, but she didn't try to move back. Their thighs glided against each other—

"How am I doing?" she asked, a little breathless, her gaze not leaving his.

The music stopped, leaving only the sound of their boots against the old wood-plank floor. He didn't want to stop. Didn't want to let go of her.

"One more dance, and you're probably good to go," he said as another song started.

She moved herself even closer and stared at his mouth. "You're easy to follow."

"That's my job. I'm easy about other things, too."

Her lips parted. "Yeah? Like what?"

"For one, listening when a pretty lady has a problem."

"What makes you think I have a problem?" she asked, her gaze lifting to meet his again.

"Intuition." He had a problem, too. A physical one, especially when she angled her body differently, pressing against his pelvis, a sparkle of something he couldn't quite define in her eyes.

"You're making me forget everything," she said.

"Is that good?"

"I'm not sure."

Time passed. Fire burned. Need intensified. "What was with the John Wayne deal?" he asked, changing subjects.

She looked away, as if deciding what to say. He waited. Patience was something he had plenty of, too. Plus, he was enjoying the hell out of dancing with her, her body close to him, all curves and temptation, his body painfully aroused as they moved around the floor, the rhythm of the music powerful and enticing. He wanted to find the nearest bed, and dance skin to skin.

"When I spotted you on the set today," she said, "I thought you looked like him. John Wayne."

"I'm taking that as a compliment."

"You should. He's my all-time favorite cowboy."

"Okay. Except I'm a cattleman. Bit of a difference. Not taking into account that he was just an actor playing a part."

The front door burst open, and a young man with a big, fancy camera came in, snapping as he went. "Look this way, Miss McShane!"

"Maybe I should get you out of here," Tony said, intending to take her out the back way.

Her fingers dug into his arms. "No," she said, almost a whisper, then louder, "no."

He tried to be her barricade again but the photographer was moving fast to get them in his frame, bypassing the men going after him.

"I'll do whatever you want, but you have to tell me," he said, more than a little curious at her wild-eyed look, like she was about to go over the edge.

"Kiss me," she said, harsh and low.

"What?" He couldn't have heard her right.

"Kiss me. Let's give them something to talk about."

"Them who?"

"Everyone. The vultures. I'm so sick of it all. So sick of always doing the right thing. Please."

Hell, he was only a man. How could he pass up an opportunity like that?

So he kissed her, a bare brush of lips, knowing it was the wrong thing to do, having seen in her eyes it was the wrong thing to do, for the wrong reasons. But reason flew out the window when his lips touched hers. He pulled her closer, looked deeper, and kissed her the way he'd wanted to since first laying eyes on her.

He heard her friends grapple with the photographer,

then the door open and close. And then everything went quiet. No music. No conversation. No pool balls.

She put her hand to her mouth. "Get me out of here. Please," she whispered, panic in her voice. She must have finally realized her mistake.

Tony didn't ask questions, but pushed her ahead of him, scooping up his hat on the way. When they reached the back parking lot, he urged her toward his truck.

"I have a car," she said, pointing. "I'll be fine."

"Are you going back to your hotel?"

"Not yet."

"Well, do you know your way around?"

"I can stop for directions…"

Even as she said it, he saw her realize she probably couldn't do that, either. It must be hell sometimes, being famous. He took over, taking her keys from her, maneuvering his big body into the driver's seat, motioning to her to get in, his knees hitting the steering wheel, even with the seat all the way back. "You can trust me. I'll take you where you want to go."

"How will you get back to get your truck?" she asked after she slammed the passenger door shut.

"Walk. Hitch. Hell, that's the least of it, don't you think?" He revved the engine and took off, heading nowhere in particular. "Who do you think that was with the camera?"

"Who knows? Someone trying to make a fast buck. Lots of people have professional cameras these days. Maybe one of those women had called someone."

So, he hadn't been her hero, after all, hadn't noticed anyone making a call, alerting someone to come and take shots—if that's what had happened.

"I can't believe I did that," she said, looking straight out the windshield.

"What? Kissed me on purpose for the camera?"

"I don't do things like that."

He knew that much about her, too, even without really knowing her. Was more than a little curious himself, but she didn't elaborate. After a few blocks with no one following, he said, "Where to?"

Her hands were clenched in her lap.

"Where're you staying?" he asked.

"I don't want to go there."

"Okay. Then where?"

"Someplace quiet."

"Not sure there are too many places where you wouldn't be recognized. And I don't have connections for private rooms and such at restaurants." He pretty much kept to himself, but he didn't tell her that. She might think he was dangerous or something.

"There," she said, pointing.

All he saw was the Red Rock Motor Inn. "The motel?"

She nodded.

"Look, I—"

"I'm not propositioning you," she interrupted. "But I'd appreciate it if you'd check in, then I'll use the room. I don't want to go back to my hotel yet. I still have some thinking to do. Would they know you here?"

He pulled into the parking lot. "By name. Some folks, anyway."

"If you pay cash, could you use an alias?"

"Don't see why not."

She reached into her pocket.

"I'll get it," he said and opened the car door before she

could protest. The woman fascinated him. What was the big deal she needed to think about? Why had she intentionally kissed him for a photographer? She had a squeaky-clean image, yet was defying it now.

He registered, climbed back into the car and drove around to the back side of the complex, parking by the assigned room. "You're registered as John Wayne," he said, slanting her a look.

She laughed, a little shaky, but still a laugh. "Thanks."

He walked her to the door, unlocked it, found the light switch. "Not what you're used to," he said as she walked past him.

"It'll do." She held out her hand. "I can't tell you how much I appreciate you helping me out. I feel horrible that you have to find your way back to your truck."

He put the car key and room key in her hand, his fingers brushing her skin, cold to the touch now. He could've left her without too much problem, knowing she'd be on his ranch the next day. But the fact was, he wasn't going anywhere. He'd taken the room next to hers for the night. "Couldn't let the Duke down, could I?"

She smiled. "The Code of the West is alive and well."

"And we're proud to say so." He tipped his hat. "Good night, then, Miss McShane." He got about six steps away when she called his name.

"It's Maggie," she said. "Call me Maggie."

"Your given name Margaret?"

"Yes."

He nodded.

"Would you…like to come in for a bit?" she asked.

He hesitated, not because he didn't want to go inside, but because he wondered what she wanted. Someone to listen? Someone to watch TV with? She didn't strike him as a person who spent a lot of time by herself. Maybe she wasn't capable of it. Maybe she was scared to be alone.

And maybe he was just too tempted by her. His body still hummed from the dance and the kiss.

"You'll be safe here," he said finally. He waited until she shut the door then went to the next room, opening the door quietly, creeping in. He didn't turn on the television, didn't make a sound, just propped himself against some pillows on the bed and read the brochures from the desktop.

The walls were thin. He heard her television come on, then go off again shortly. He heard her move around the room. Television on again. Off. She must not have bothered taking off her boots because he could hear her pace. Finally a new sound—crying. Then she told herself to stop it, and she did. No more sobs.

Vulnerable. He wouldn't have put that word to her if he hadn't seen it for himself.

She paced again. And the crying started again. He couldn't stand it any longer. He went outside and tapped on her door. "It's Tony," he said quietly.

The curtain moved. He put himself in a position where she could see him. Then the door opened.

"Couldn't you get a ride?" she asked.

He could see she was giving it her all to appear calm and composed. But for all her acting abilities, the look she gave him was anything but.

"Didn't try. I wasn't comfortable with leaving you here alone. Took the room next door. I could hear you—pacing. Figured, you know, maybe you might want to talk."

She opened the door wider and stepped back, extending her invitation a second time, silently.

He took off his hat and went into the room, heard the door shut and the lock slide into place, then the chain being fastened. He tossed his hat onto the bed, a typical motel queen-size with a muted-stripes bedspread that had seen better days. Sterile room, usual odors of cleaning products and stale fabrics. He'd spent plenty of nights in ones just like this or worse. He'd bet she hadn't.

He faced her. She hadn't moved. And where her composure had failed when she'd answered the door, it was back now. She was a damn fine actress, he decided, to be able to make her face a blank like that. What was going on in her head? Why was he there?

"How can I help you?" he asked.

She tossed back her hair a little, bringing her chin up a notch. "I want to sleep with you."

A stampede started in his midsection then branched out. He tried for as little expression as she had. "For the sake of clarification, 'sleeping' with me means?"

"More than actually sleeping in the same bed."

"You want to have sex?"

"Yes."

More questions came to mind. In particular, *Why me?* And, *What about your famous fiancé?*

Their kiss in the saloon reverberated in his head, made its way down his body. Who was he to pass up a once-in-a-lifetime opportunity? The kind of guy who realized that maybe she didn't mean what she was saying, he thought.

But then she started to pull the snaps on her shirt apart. He stopped her, his hand covering both of hers, his fingers pressed to her warm, cushiony chest.

"Some reason why you're in such an all-fired-up hurry?" he asked.

"Yes." She yanked her shirt open, revealing a lacy red bra cupping not-girl-next-door breasts.

Usually he took his time to do things right. Less chance of regrets that way. And somehow he had a feeling that regrets were going to come fast and furious if he followed through. No way was he going to do this, even though it had been a while since he'd enjoyed a roll in the hay. But this woman had been occupying his thoughts for several days and nights, pretty much since he saw her walk onto his ranch a few days ago, and the moment she touched her lips to his, pressed herself against him, he was lost.

Her kisses seared him, her touch sent him soaring. He lost his ability to think clearly. They wasted no time in undressing and getting skin to skin on the bed. She was wild and demanding and giving. He barely managed to say, "Birth control?"

"On the pill," she managed back.

And then he was inside her and she was arching and digging her fingers into him and making flattering sounds of pleasure, and then of satisfaction. A moment later, he did, too.

He eased to his side, taking her along. After a minute he realized she was crying. Again.

He didn't ask her why, and she didn't say.

Tony's internal alarm clock woke him before dawn. He reached for Maggie, but his hand landed on a piece of paper instead of a warm, curvy body. He held the paper toward the window, where the outside light offered minimal illumination.

One word, printed as if in a rush: *Thanks*.

It should've made him happy, since he wasn't much for mornings-after, either, but it only annoyed him.

He rolled off the bed and snagged his cell phone out of his jeans pocket, then called his foreman, Butch Kelly.

"I need a ride," Tony said.

"Where are you?"

Tony could hear the rustle of clothing as Butch dressed. "Red Rock Motor Inn. Know where it is?"

"Spent my high-school graduation night there. Fond memories. So, where's your truck?"

"Elsewhere."

A beat passed then, "Okay. I'm on my way."

Tony hung up and finished dressing. It was hard to believe she'd left without him hearing her go. He wondered how long ago she'd taken off. Sometime after three, because that was when they'd made love a second time.

He waited for Butch in front of the motel, his irritation increasing with each passing vehicle. Her note burned a hole in his shirt pocket. She could've said goodbye, at least. People who sleep together deserve that much.

She obviously didn't deserve her driven-snow reputation—supposedly she was engaged to that Hollywood beefcake. She sure hadn't acted engaged last night. In fact, she'd seemed like a woman who hadn't been made love to in a long time. He wondered about that, and about her morals, sleeping with him like she had.

But, hell, who was he to spout morals? He'd had his share of affairs, some that never should've happened.

He tucked his hands in his pockets, and hunched against the cool morning, remembering. She was amazing in bed. He wouldn't mind repeating the experience, not at all. Yeah, why not have some good times together while she was in town? They'd be private about it. He didn't want or need media attention, and she would need secrecy from her fiancé. Could be tricky, though.

Where the hell was Butch, anyway?

He blew out a long breath, digging for the patience he was known for. It was probably just karma catching up with him, payback for the times in his youth he'd done the same thing, left a woman without saying goodbye, before he'd wised up and gotten civil about such things.

A Lucky Hand Ranch pickup pulled up to the curb. "Took you long enough," Tony muttered as he climbed in, not feeling charitable, too much on his mind.

Butch shoved a to-go cup at him. Coffee, hot and black. "So, shoot me. Figured you'd need this, so I made a stop."

They were the same age, had done the rodeo circuit together for years. Butch's knees were worse than Tony's, although Tony had broken more bones. "Okay. You're forgiven," Tony said.

Butch grinned. "So, can I ask what you were doin' at the motel?"

Tony gave him a long look as he sipped his coffee. His cell rang. He checked to see who it was. "Pretty early, Mom, even for you," he said after he opened the phone.

Sue-Ellen Young laughed. "I've already baked two pies and checked my e-mail. Nice picture of you, by the way, on celebrityscoop.com, kissing Maggie McShane."

And so it began, Tony thought. But how would it end?

Chapter Three

Maggie's stomach lurched as she focused on the computer screen being shoved close to her face.

"Tell me this is a look-alike," Leesa almost screamed. She'd stomped into Maggie's hotel suite a minute ago, holding up her laptop. "One of those fake celebrities. Tell me that."

Embarrassed by her behavior, Maggie picked up her purse and headed toward the door. "It's not a look-alike."

"How did this happen? *When* did it happen?"

"Last night. Are you ready to go? You know I don't like being late to the set. Dino's got the car waiting." When she'd gotten back to her hotel room around 4:00 a.m. she'd had to memorize the day's lines, meaning she'd had little sleep, only the two hours between the first and second time she and Tony had made love. Her makeup artist was going to get after her for the bags under her eyes.

"How can you be so blasé about this? You're engaged! You were caught kissing a local cowboy at a *bar!*" She grabbed script pages and a couple other items off the table.

"Cattleman."

Leesa stopped in her tracks. "What?"

"He's a cattleman. He says there's a difference." It was costing Maggie to act unconcerned by the online-gossip site's photo, but she had to. Until she came up with a plan, she had to seem as if she knew what she was doing. Appearances were everything. She didn't want to compound stupidity with idiocy.

"I don't get it," Leesa said, exasperated. "Last night Scott was here. You asked for privacy for the whole night, just the two of you. What happened?"

They stepped onto the landing. Maggie put a hand on her friend's arm. "The less you know, the better. For your sake, not mine, okay? You're just going to have to trust me. I want you to be able to say it was a big surprise to you, too, and mean it."

Leesa clamped her mouth hard for a minute, then said, "So, the rumors about Scott were true."

"What rumors?"

"That he and Gennifer were messing around."

So. Even Leesa had known. "Had you planned to tell me?" Maggie asked, hurt making her throat burn.

"They were only rumors. I'd been trying to get them confirmed, but no luck. I wouldn't have let you marry him without telling you, Mags. Did you know already? Did you call it off?"

Dino pulled up in the car and got out. Maggie couldn't tell from his expression if he knew about the photo, but he didn't hold out his hand for her to pass him her engagement ring as he always did, which told her enough.

"You all right?" he asked.

"Just super."

"You know, if you don't trust me, you should fire me."

She jerked back. "I trust you."

"I wouldn't have let anyone get a picture, and I don't pass judgment. You shouldn't leave me behind."

"I had to." She couldn't tell him any more than that. Not yet.

"I'll keep your secrets until the day I die, Maggie."

She felt about a foot tall. How many people had she disappointed or hurt with her impulsive actions?

"Thank you, Dino. I do know that." She climbed into the car and said to Leesa, "Let's run lines."

Leesa huffed but pulled out the pages.

At the location, Maggie went straight into hair and makeup. She'd barely settled into the chair when Mac Iverson came in. "Give us a few minutes," the director said to the two women working on her, then he leaned against the counter and gave her the eye. "So. You're big news today."

She assumed that meant her photo was everywhere now. Her manager and publicist would already be fielding calls from the various media entertainment-news shows, and magazines, too. Leesa would be fielding calls from her manager and publicist, and any others who had her phone number.

"I'm sorry," Maggie said to Mac. She never brought controversy to a film. Mac wouldn't work with her if she did. He was old-school, running a close-knit, familylike atmosphere, but demanding and getting the best work out of everyone. They'd worked together six times. There were good reasons for that.

"I met Tony Young for the first time last year when we were scouting locations," Mac said. "I wanted realism, not a studio set. At the time he was living in the old homestead we're shooting in, but his new house was almost ready. He agreed to hold off on remodeling the old place for his foreman until after we filmed, appreciating what I promised to bring to the movie—an honest portrayal of a cattleman's life, not the romanticized version of most fiction. He's a decent, hardworking, self-made man. He shouldn't have to deal with the kind of media attention he's bound to get now."

Maggie felt like a child being chewed out by her favorite teacher, except…shouldn't Tony take some of blame? She hadn't acted alone. "I know."

"Have you and Scott broken your engagement?"

"Yes."

He closed his eyes for a moment. "Okay. Good. That's good. And is Mr. Young in the picture now?"

Maggie realized right then what she needed to do, how she needed to resolve the situation. She had to talk to Tony first, however. "Can I just say that I'll issue a statement later today and leave it at that for the moment?"

"Is this going to interfere with my production?"

"I'm trying not to let it, Mac. I'm sorry that it's considered newsworthy."

"Yeah, well, if you weren't such a Goody Two-shoes…" He smiled then and pushed himself from the counter. "Wonder what the clever headline writers will do with America's Sweetheart now."

"If it makes them stop using that awful nickname, it might all be worth it. It's been pretty hard to live up to, you know."

"Not while your grandparents were alive."

She finally smiled. "True. They did keep me on the straight and narrow, whether I wanted to be or not."

Mac patted her shoulder then left. When she was finished in hair and makeup she headed to her trailer to get into costume. Leesa popped up off the sofa, her cell phone to her ear.

"She's here," she said into the phone. "Hang on." Leesa held out the phone to her. "It's Garnet."

Garnet Halvorsen had been Maggie's publicist for ten years, ever since Maggie lured her away from a big studio. She should've been the first call Maggie had made once she'd seen the photograph.

"I'll call her later," Maggie said. She kept walking, her dresser coming into the trailer behind her with the outfit for the morning's shoot.

"But—"

"*La*-ter."

Maggie heard Leesa try to soothe Garnet, who seemed to be yelling. Maggie signaled to her assistant to end the call, which she did. "Let it go to voice mail for now, please, Leesa."

A few minutes later someone knocked, saying they were ready for her. Maggie put an arm around Leesa's shoulders. "Everything's going to be fine."

Maggie wanted to believe her own words, but it really depended on Tony. "I need you to get in touch with Tony Young and ask him to meet me at seven o'clock tonight at the hotel. And apologize to him in advance for all the stalkers he'll have today."

"I don't mind making that call, Mags, but don't you

think it should come from you? That any apology should come from you?"

Without a doubt. But since he would have questions that she'd rather answer in person, she hoped he would agree to come. Needed him to come. Her reputation depended on it, although he owed her nothing.

"Please just make the call." Maggie opened the trailer door, her stomach full of hot lead, especially about Tony's life being turned upside down, but she put on her game face and headed out to the set.

The tone now was completely different from previous days. She always got along with everyone, but she'd never been involved in a scandal before, and no one seemed to know what to say or how to act, except that cameraman Pete came up, allegedly to give her some change from the fifty dollars she'd given the bartender, then whispered to her that he could call Scott and tell him that it had all been innocent between Maggie and the cowboy.

Innocent? Not by a long shot, but Maggie was touched by Pete's loyalty. She politely declined, more guilt pressing on her.

Once *action* was called, everyone got down to business, and the morning flew by. They were filming inside the old homestead. She tried to picture Tony there, wondered how much had been changed for the movie. Necessary people and equipment filled the space, not as small as it looked from the outside. Which bedroom had Tony slept in? Where was his new house? He must own a lot of acres not to have another house visible on the horizon, although other ranch structures were in sight.

And where were the cattle? It was a cattle ranch, after

all, and she hadn't spotted one, not even on the long, beautiful drive in and out each day.

Between takes she looked to Leesa for a signal that she'd reached Tony, but she shook her head each time. At the end of the day, Maggie was tempted to get directions to his new house and go there personally, except that she'd probably have to battle paparazzi, unless Tony had figured out a way to get rid of them.

At least the set was closed, and the passenger windows on her car were tinted, so Dino should be able to get her back to the hotel without being followed. Maybe. Mac had already upped the number of security people. Dino was talking about bringing in extra security of his own. She left the decision to him.

Why hadn't Tony returned Leesa's call? How furious was he? Or maybe embarrassed was a better word. If he wouldn't come to her, how could she get to *him?* She didn't think she could handle this…*situation* over the phone, but a personal plea via telephone to come see her might be the only way to get him. She didn't want to make assumptions about why he hadn't called. He may not even be at home, and she didn't have his cell phone number—and didn't want to ask Mac for it. His residence number, amazingly, was listed in the directory.

On top of that, she and Scott had played phone tag all day, but with both of them actively filming, they hadn't caught each other during downtimes. She preferred to wait to talk to him until she'd met with Tony, anyway, so that'd been okay.

Maggie managed to keep working all day, presenting a happy face until she stepped into her hotel shower at the end of the day. In the privacy of that space she broke down, giving in to the overwhelming emotions of the past twenty-four hours, first Scott breaking up with her, then sleeping with a man she barely knew, then her reputation taking a major hit of her own making, along with the reputation of a man innocent of such treatment, when all he'd done was rescue her.

No one's reputation had ever suffered because of her actions. Until now.

"Maggie?" Leesa called through the bathroom door. "Mr. Young is here."

So. He'd shown up at seven o'clock, just as she'd asked. He just hadn't bothered to let her know he was coming. "Okay. I'll be out in a few minutes. Offer him something to drink, please."

Maggie turned off the shower, made quick work of drying off then slipped into cropped pants and a sleeveless top. She towel-dried her hair, put on a little lip gloss, screwed up her courage, and went to greet him.

Well, damn, she'd wanted him here at seven, he got here at seven, and she was in the shower? Some consideration. Movie stars. Who needs 'em?

Tony stood at the living-room window, his hands shoved into his pockets, and looked out at the view. The sunset colors were brilliant but fading fast.

He'd had a helluva day, had been badgered by his sister, both brothers and just about everyone else who knew his phone number. He'd stopped answering around 10:00 a.m. There were eighteen messages he hadn't returned, didn't plan on returning. Of his family, only his father hadn't weighed in, but Tony figured he'd hear something before too long. Hoyt Young always had an opinion on how his youngest son was living his life, and

the fact it looked like Tony had been entertaining someone else's fiancée wouldn't sit well with his highly moral
father.

Hell, it didn't sit well with Tony, either, high morals
or otherwise.

"I'm so sorry to keep you waiting," came Maggie's
voice from behind him. "I didn't know you were coming
or I would've been ready."

He angled toward her, was surprised to see her dressed
so casually. Her hair was wet, leaving damp spots where
it touched her blouse. She was barefoot. She looked ready
to bolt, too—nervous and fidgety.

"I was ordered to be here at seven," he said.

"I hope that's not true. I hope Leesa extended an invitation for you to come, not ordered you."

"It may have been politely stated, but it wasn't a question."

"Then I apologize. Leesa was pretty frazzled this morning, fielding the frenzy to our photograph, which I assume
you saw?"

"My mother let me know this morning around four-thirty."

"Your— I'm so sorry. Please, would you have a seat?
Did Leesa get you something to drink?"

"I'm fine, thanks." He sat in a leather chair. She perched
on the edge of the sofa, as if incapable of settling back or
relaxing. Her fingers were interlocked. He remembered
how she'd cried last night....

"Were the paparazzi hounding you?" she asked.

"They tried. I made sure they didn't follow me here." It
had actually been fun ducking them, but he wouldn't want
it on a regular basis.

"I owe you an explanation," she said.

"I'm all ears."

"Please understand that I'm going to tell you things I haven't told anyone else. Even though I've turned your world upside down, I'm asking for your discretion. I know I have no right to ask but—"

"I know how to keep my mouth shut."

She closed her eyes a moment. Her vulnerability hit him hard. Like last night, he wanted to protect her, even though he didn't know from what. He could easily be a fool for this woman.

"I assume by now you know I was engaged to Scott Gibson," she said.

"Hard to miss that bit of information."

"What no one else knows is that he broke it off yesterday. He was here waiting for me after shooting. He said he'd fallen in love with someone else."

Which answered a lot of Tony's questions about why she'd slept with him last night—and why she'd been crying. "I'm sorry."

"Thanks." She looked at her lap. "Okay. Biggest confidence now. I'm not sorry. Scott even said as he was leaving that someday I would be happy about it. That someday came a lot faster than I would've thought. It came today."

"How can you get over it that fast?"

"I know it sounds heartless, and the rest of what I'm going to tell you won't put me in a good light, either, but you deserve the truth, after all the trouble I've caused you." She pushed herself up, moved to stand at the window.

He found he couldn't sit still, either, so he joined her.

"It's an incredible landscape, isn't it?" she asked, apparently stalling. "Not lush but starkly beautiful, especially here, surrounded by the enormous red rocks."

"Most beautiful in the whole country."

"You've traveled a lot?"

"I did the rodeo circuit for about twelve years. It's a nomadic kind of life. When it was time to settle down, there was no place for me but here."

She nodded. "I'm looking to settle down myself."

He waited, knowing she was working up to what she needed to say.

"It's why I was marrying Scott. I wanted a home. Some stability."

"You didn't love him?"

"It's…complicated."

"I've got nothin' but time, Margaret."

"So, you've decided to call me Margaret? Trying to be different?"

"I'm thinking Margaret suits you." Maggie was who the world saw—strong and feisty. Margaret was vulnerable…and passionate.

She met his gaze and smiled a little. He ignored the tug inside his chest.

"Scott and I met when we were set up to attend a premiere together by our mutual agent and our publicists. It wasn't the first time I'd done such a thing. It's part of the job, good publicity for both parties, yada, yada. But things clicked between Scott and me. We liked each other right away and started dating, as much as our situations allowed. We discovered one of the biggest things we had in common was that we'd both lost our parents at a young age. My grandparents had taken me in, raised me with a very strict upbringing, one I didn't rebel from. He'd grown up in the foster system. We were both searching for a fantasy life, I think."

"I think we all do that," he said, glad to see she'd calmed some.

"You, too?"

"Of course. I was even married once. One big fantasy, that's for sure. Ended with a hard dose of reality." He hardly ever thought about her anymore, it had been so long. A man who didn't put the past behind him couldn't move forward. He'd been bitter for a while, but time had cured that, too.

"Well, Scott understood the pressures of the business, as well as the media, of course. One night he asked me to marry him and I said yes, figuring we had a better-than-average chance for success, since we had similar backgrounds."

"You didn't love him? He didn't love you?"

"We each said so, but looking back, I don't know. I think we got caught up in the romance of it all. And then before we had time to sit back and reconsider, our publicity machines went into overdrive and the whole world was involved."

"You could've backed out. Better that than make a bigger mistake."

She turned around, leaned against the window frame and finally looked at him. "Of course you're right. But by then an old friend of mine, Jenny Warren, had called and asked a big favor. Her family is about to open two luxury hotels, The Taka San Francisco and The Taka Kyoto. The San Francisco opening is scheduled for around the end of September. Jenny asked if I'd hold the wedding there, have a huge, lavish event. They'd assumed all costs. I could just tell them what I want, and it would be done. Publicity for everyone. Win-win, right? Scott wanted the big splash, too, so I said yes. And regretted it right away. 'Big' isn't my style."

"So you felt stuck?"

"I never put that word to it. I felt…rushed. But then I had this movie to film, and Scott had his, so there wasn't time to hash it out."

"In all the headlines I read today, I didn't see anything about your engagement being over, only that you were caught kissing a cowboy. In fact, nothing from your…Scott at all."

"That's because I told him I needed a couple of days to figure out how to handle it. Then instead of staying home and working it out alone, I handled it by taking myself to a cowboy bar and dancing with a tall, dark and handsome cattleman. And then kissing him so that a photographer could film it." She put a hand on his chest, lightly, briefly, and smiled.

"At least no one knows about us sharing a motel room," he said. "I'm sure my foreman, who came to get me, put two and two together, but he won't say a word." He finally gave in to the need to touch her and brushed her hair back from her face with his fingertips. He wouldn't mind hauling her off to her bedroom. Wouldn't mind it at all.

"I'm so sorry for all the trouble this has caused you, Tony."

Hell, his family's admiration of him had gone up a notch or two. It was a shame that's what it took for them to see how successful he was. He'd built his ranch from almost nothing, making it what it was today. He was damn proud of it. He still had a ways to go, but he'd done it himself— mostly, anyway. He had something to prove, especially to his father, but sleeping with a movie star wasn't how he'd envisioned proving himself.

"Well, now, Margaret," Tony said, putting on the cowboy act thick for her, "seems to me I got somethin' special to keep in my memory out of it. I can live with people teasin' me." He leaned in to kiss her.

"Could you live with it for a few more months?" she asked before their lips touched.

He pulled back, met her gaze, saw that her jitters were back. "Meaning?"

"Last night when I said I knew who you were, that you owned the ranch, you said your ranch owns you. Am I remembering that right?"

"You are."

She drew a deep breath. "Okay. So, then, I have a proposition for you."

The last one had resulted in their being naked together. If this one involved that again, he'd be saying yes faster than a bronc bursts out of a chute.

"I'm listenin', darlin'."

"Marry me."

Chapter Four

Maggie watched him let the words sink in. She made herself remember to breathe.

His astonishment came through in his voice. "Marry you? Why in hell would I do that? I've known you for about the lifespan of a mayfly."

"It wouldn't be for forever. A few months, maybe."

"I repeat—why in hell would I do that?"

"Because I'll make it worth your while."

"Darlin', all the sex in the world isn't worth being leg-shackled to a Hollywood star. Even sex as good as last night's."

She smiled. "It *was* good, wasn't it?"

"Hell, yes, it was good. You know that. You sure don't need me puffin' up your ego about it. But it wasn't 'I-do' good."

"As much as I appreciate the compliments, Tony, I

wasn't offering sex as a way of making it worth your while. I'm offering money."

His eyes went hard, so did his jaw. Apparently she'd insulted him.

"According to what I've heard," she hurried on, "the cattle business is tenuous, always in need of more capital to keep it thriving. I'll buy whatever you need for the ranch, in exchange for a short-term marriage."

"*Whatever* I need?"

"A man like you wouldn't ask for more than what's fair."

He walked away from her, headed to the well-stocked bar. "I think I'd like that drink now."

She gave him space to think, waited as he poured himself something straight up. Whiskey? Scotch? She couldn't see the label on the bottle. He downed two fingers of whatever he was having, poured another, then let it sit as he leaned on the bar.

"And just how do you plan to spin such a thing for the media?" he asked.

He hadn't said no. Not outright. That was good, wasn't it? "I figure if I just say we met and fell in love, that it just happened, catching us completely off guard, and that Scott has been wonderfully understanding, it'll do."

"So, he comes out of it scot-free, pardon the pun? He falls for another woman while you're engaged, breaks up with you and you're going to take all the heat? I don't get it."

"I would be saving face from being dumped."

"So, it's better for you to look silly and frivolous than be dumped by some jerk? You're not convincing me."

"I know the logic is flawed to you, but in my business, it's about image. Everyone loves a love story. The public will forgive me, because it's my first misstep. They wouldn't have forgiven Scott so easily."

"You want to protect him after what he did?"

"No. I just don't want this to become the scandal of the year. It can be spun right. You and I met. We fell in love. It was a force bigger than us. People will eat it up. But besides that, I'd also be keeping my commitment to my friend to have the wedding at The Taka, which is very important, too. I keep my promises, Tony. And I know it seems like a ridiculous solution to you, but I've given it a lot of thought. It's the best choice for me." She came up to him at the bar. "You don't owe me any favors. I know all I've done is mess up your life, and it will only get messier if you say yes. There will be a media uproar the likes of which you've never experienced. And all you get out of this is cold, hard cash."

"What about sex?" Tony didn't know whether to smile or not at her expression, as if it hadn't even occurred to her.

"What about it?" she finally asked.

"Is it part of the deal?" He figured the reason she'd slept with him the night before was that she was hurting and wanted to forget the pain.

"Do you want it to be part of the deal?" she asked.

He understood then that it hadn't been him personally she'd wanted, but that fate had brought them together, and there was a certain amount of attraction, maybe more on his part than hers. "It would be tricky, don't you think?" he said. "In order to make the marriage look real, we're going to have to sleep in the same bed. We can't trust anyone other than ourselves to keep the real reasons secret."

"I agree."

"Do you think we can sleep in the same bed and not make love?" he pressed.

"We only have to get through a couple of months. People aren't surprised when Hollywood marriages end quickly. It seems to me we'd be complicating things a lot if we were having sex along the way, too."

So, he really had been a means to an end last night. Still was, for that matter. "If such things are accepted as easily as you say, why are you asking *me?* You could have your choice of dozens of men, I imagine."

"We're already linked or the idea wouldn't even have occurred to me. I would've bitten the bullet and announced that Scott and I had broken up. Without you, that's what'll happen, even though the world has seen us kissing."

"There's got to be more to it than that, Margaret. You wouldn't put yourself in legal proximity with me—and in my bed every night—just because we've already been linked."

Maggie laid a hand on his, resting on the counter, and met his gaze. "I've already figured out you're trustworthy. I need someone who can keep a secret, and I believe you're that man. You didn't boast about us sleeping together. A lot of men would've."

"Okay," he said.

She went still. "Really? You're saying yes?"

"Yes."

"Why?"

"Like you, my answers wouldn't be logical," he said. "And so I'm keeping 'em to myself. Does it matter, anyway?"

"I told you my secrets."

"You also flat-out told me you needed someone who can keep secrets."

After a moment she laughed.

"I'm chivalrous," he said. "That's all you need to know."

Her cell phone rang, and she jumped. She'd left the

phone on the coffee table behind her. "That could be Scott," she said haltingly. "I should answer it. We need to—"

"Get the details worked out," Tony said, finishing her sentence as she took a step back. He picked up his glass and took a sip. "Go right ahead."

She answered the phone then mouthed Scott's name. Tony took his glass and wandered to the window again, listening to her talk to her ex-fiancé, figuring out a game plan, which involved agents, managers, publicists, trusted journalists and others, as if they were making a big business deal.

He heard her say, "The less you know about him, the better," which made Tony make eye contact with her. "I'm marrying him. That's all you need to know. Hey, you're coming out the good guy here, so just drop it, okay?"

Tony lifted his glass to her then took a sip.

His gut reaction to her proposal had been to say no. He'd changed his mind because he never backed away from conflict or controversy. After turning forty last month, he'd come to realize how dissatisfied he was, had always been. As the youngest of four, he'd forever been playing catch-up to his brothers, always pushing to match or surpass their success, even back in his rodeo days. Expectations had been high for him, the pressure enormous.

Instead of falling in step, however, he'd bucked the system—and his family—and had become the black sheep, rebellious, even antisocial to a degree.

The second he'd graduated from high school, he'd hit the rodeo circuit, avoiding going home to visit or even calling. He'd gone into it angry, because his father hadn't believed in him, so Tony had focused on winning and little else. It was no wonder his marriage had failed. He'd needed to create a new family for himself. He failed at it. Yeah, way to prove to his father he was a winner.

Not that women still hadn't been drawn to him, but he never kept any of them around for long, sometimes their choice, most times his.

So he'd decided he needed to make a change in his life, even before Maggie McShane had come along. He wasn't sure he could've asked for a bigger change than marrying her. And since it wasn't going to be a real commitment, the plan was exactly suited to him, something to jump-start his new life. Maybe this famous, beautiful movie star wasn't exactly what he'd had in mind as a change, but she'd do.

"That's done, then," Maggie said, snapping her phone shut. "I need to talk with my publicist. She'll take care of the details. Will you be available for a press conference tomorrow? I think we should do this in person and let people see us together making goo-goo eyes at each other, rather than issuing a statement for someone else to read."

"Goo-goo eyes?"

She laughed. "You know what I mean."

"I'm supposed to look like I'm sweet on you. Got it." He paused. "I've got one condition to this whole business, Margaret."

She lost her smile. Wariness dulled her eyes. "What's that?"

"I'll be the one to decide when to end the marriage, not you."

"Why?"

"Because you're running this entire show, otherwise. Doesn't sit well with me."

"It's a big condition."

"Take it or leave it." He needed control over something

in this whole business, especially the right to end things if it all turned sour sooner than expected.

She stuck out her hand. "Deal."

"And a prenup," he added.

"Also a deal."

He took her hand and pulled her close. He'd never really answered her question about them sharing a bed, only *she* had. He had no intention of having a sexless marriage to this sexy woman, but he knew he needed to woo her. She'd acted out of hurt last night. He didn't want her again unless it was *him* she was wanting.

Just him.

"Normally a handshake'd do it for me, but not this time." He'd been waiting all night to kiss her again, wondering if reality matched the fantasy floating around in his head all day. He gave it his all, wanting to remind her of last night, too. He didn't let her hold back but demanded the passion he knew was inside her. He heard her moan, felt her mouth open more, and her fingers dig into him. The same heat he'd felt before flared again. It wasn't a fantasy. She was real. And she wanted him just as much as he wanted her. Not sleep together? Like hell. One way or another he was going to end up where they started.

"Maggie," came a woman's voice. "Oh! Oh, I'm so sorry." Maggie's assistant turned tail.

"What is it, Leesa?" Maggie asked, easing free of him.

"Garnet just landed in Phoenix. We're supposed to powwow, I gather."

"Garnet's my publicist," Maggie said to Tony. "We'll probably be up a good part of the night working out the details. She's fast on her feet, though. You can stay, if you want, or I can fill you in tomorrow."

He gathered he wasn't being invited to spend the night here at the hotel.

"I'm sorry," she said quietly, her hand on his arm. "I've also got lines to learn tonight."

"I think I'll stay a spell and see how the wheels turn in your business." A smart man learned everything he could so as to not look the fool. "But, Margaret—you'll be moving into my house tomorrow at the end of the day."

She didn't say anything for a long, tense moment, then she turned to Leesa, whose eyes went wide at their conversation. Just wait until she heard they were getting married. "We're going to need food, Leesa. And once Garnet arrives, I'll need you and Dino to join us, too, so get enough food for five."

"Oh. Okay." She left, then Maggie said, "Let's sit down."

He could do that. He just wasn't going to change his mind. She would move to his house or else. "I'm not moving in with you here," he said as they sat on the sofa.

"I don't expect you to. But me moving in with you isn't a quick and easy task. I have staff that have to be accommodated. Security arrangements to be made."

"Staff? How many?"

"I'm traveling light at the moment. Just Leesa and Dino. And Garnet now, of course, but she can stay here at the hotel. I hope she won't need to hang around long."

"Who's Dino?"

"The head of my security, and for this trip, my driver. Because of all the hoopla, he's called three others of his crew here. They'll need to be put up."

"I can find room for Leesa. As for Dino and the rest— I guard my own."

She frowned. "You'd be spending every minute chasing

people off, and they'd still find ways to get close. Really, Tony, you have no idea what you're in for."

"Then I'll hire my own people."

She set a hand on his thigh. "Dino would just as soon spend the night in a sleeping bag on your porch than not be close enough to guard me. No, don't say anything yet. Please let me finish. I understand your man-need to take care of me. But it's been Dino's job for ten years. He won't back down. And you two really have to get along. It's important. I'm comfortable with him, Tony. Doesn't that count?"

She didn't get it, Tony thought. There could be only one boss in any given situation. In this one, he was it.

"I'll work it out with him." He stood. If he sat there another second he was going to haul her to the bedroom, and that wasn't allowed. Yet. "You said you had lines to learn? Why don't you work on those until your publicist gets here. I wouldn't mind watching the Diamondbacks game. I don't need sound for that."

He didn't give her a chance to say no but grabbed the remote, turned on the huge-screen TV and plunked himself into a big leather chair. Out of the corner of his eye he saw when she finally moved, going to a console table and grabbing a stack of papers.

She paced, gesturing, speaking too quietly to hear the words. He tried to act interested in the game. He couldn't have cared less, much as he loved his D-backs.

An assortment of food was delivered. She didn't stop, continuing to memorize while eating and walking at the same time.

He was a little worried about her. The first time he'd seen her on set a few days ago, she'd looked rested and happy. Now she looked…older, and there were channels between her brows that he'd bet anything she'd been taught forever to avoid. Frown lines were, well, frowned on in her line of work. Just his guess, anyway. He knew she hadn't gotten much sleep the night before, and wouldn't tonight. He might have to step in and handle things.

The next time the door opened, in came a guy taller than Tony's own six foot four who carried a solid fifty pounds more. His head was shaved. He wore a suit and tie, even in the Arizona heat. There wasn't a visible drop of sweat on him. The famous Dino, Tony figured.

Beside him was a black-haired, green-eyed, size-two woman, maybe a few years older than Maggie, but sophisticated in ways Maggie wasn't. There was just something edgy about her... He wasn't sure what to make of her.

"Oh, my God. Food. Thank you, thank you," she said, heading to the dining table. "I recognize you," she said to Tony. "You're the cowboy who changed our world."

"Garnet Halvorsen," Maggie said, "meet Tony Young. My fiancé."

Chapter Five

No one could accuse Garnet of underreacting, Maggie thought moments after introducing Tony. Garnet went ballistic, instantly, magnificently, storming around the room, uttering dire warnings of career-altering backlash for jumping from one man to the next in the span of a day. Maggie let her rant, knowing she needed to get it out of her system.

Leesa, on the other hand, just fixed herself a sandwich and ate.

Dino's expression didn't change.

"I know we've just met, Ms. Halvorsen," Tony interrupted, probably reaching the end of his patience, "but would you please just sit down and let's talk about this. I don't see how you're doin' any good here."

Maggie could've kissed him. A cool head should prevail, and she was glad it was his, glad he wasn't a man who would just go along. Her admiration of him notched a little higher.

Maggie sat in the dining chair that Tony held for her. The others followed suit, even Dino, although he had to be ordered. He was happiest standing on the fringes, whether the event was big or small.

"First," Tony said, taking Maggie's hand, "Maggie didn't jump from one man to the next in a day. She did her best to resist. But, frankly, once I saw her, I was determined to have her. And that was that."

Maggie kept her shock to herself. If he wanted to handle the situation this way, who was she to complain? Chivalrous, indeed, if also a tad arrogant. She liked him even more.

"I'm confused," Garnet said. "Didn't you two just meet, like, yesterday?"

"So it would seem to the world," he said. "Actually we met before that. No one needs to know the details. She rebuffed me, even flashed her ring at me, but I got pushy. I'm not known for my patience."

Maggie clamped her lips against the laughter that threatened. "Patience" certainly was a strong suit of his.

Garnet looked at Maggie then. "Okay. Love conquers all, and all that crap. But couldn't you have ended the engagement with Scott, given it a few weeks and *then* gone public with your new love?"

"If the photo hadn't hit the airwaves, we could have and would have," Maggie said. "But we weren't given that option, and now there has to be an explanation, right? Otherwise people will think I was cheating on Scott. My engagement with Scott was already over when the picture was taken." She felt Tony squeeze her hand in encouragement.

"So, what are your plans? I need details, because people will want details."

"The wedding will go on as scheduled, except with a different groom. Scott will give his own statement, saying he's happy for me, that he only wants the best for me, yada, yada. Tony and I will hold a press conference and issue our own statement, then we'll field a few questions. You can prearrange those with some people you trust, right, Garnet?"

"Of course. Listen, are you sure about having the wedding? Because if *this* wedding doesn't stick, you're risking your future. Your career was built on your good-girl image, on and off the screen—an easy thing to pull off because it was true. Tarnish doesn't make for good box-office receipts, and you're young enough to enjoy another ten years of the lucrative roles you've had."

"People also love a great romance, Garnet. This is the kind of stuff my movies are made of. I don't think it'll hurt. Not this one time, anyway."

"Maybe." Garnet slanted a look at Tony. "What's your background? What kind of dirt will the press gather on you? And tell me the truth. I can only take care of what I know."

"I was a pro rodeo rider for twelve years, did well enough to get myself inducted into the ProRodeo Hall of Fame a while back after winning the All-Around Cowboy five times."

"What does that mean?"

"That I was the top-dollar winner in two or more events each of those years."

"So, there's money in rodeoing?"

"I did okay. Made more on endorsements."

"Like any other sport."

"Yep. I won my spread in a poker game. It came with a

manure-load of hard work, and I'm breaking even now most years. Was married once, a long time ago. She left me for a Philadelphia banker and a better life. I have a big family, a simple life and a lot of memories, some good, some not. I sowed plenty of oats, but that's in my past. I think I'm pretty ordinary."

Maggie learned more about him in that one little speech than she'd known. It was boggling to think she was committed to marrying someone she knew so little about. But, ordinary? Nope. He was far from ordinary.

"And you love Maggie?" Garnet asked.

The room went quiet. He lifted their clasped hands and kissed her fingers. "She's everything."

"You're not answering the question. Believe me, people much tougher than me are going to ask it."

"And I'll tell 'em to just look at us and decide for themselves. The words we say to each other aren't for public consumption. Her private life's gonna be just that."

He would present himself well to the press, Maggie thought. She didn't need to worry about that at all. She did need to worry about his fantasy that her—their—private life would stay private. Apparently he was going to have to find out the hard way that it wasn't in the realm of possibility.

"Maggie and I want as much normalcy as we can manage," Tony said, "given her star status and the public interest in her personal affairs. We'll be available for the one press conference tomorrow. After that, we're done."

Garnet shook her head. "I'll have interview requests from the networks, cable, plus print media the moment you announce your engagement. You'll have to choose *some*one. Scott's waiting for you to talk first, before he says anything, right?"

"Yes, and Tony and I will discuss each potential inter-view and make up our minds together," Maggie answered, knowing Tony would just keep refusing. "Garnet, you said you were starved, so let's eat and relax, then we'll finish up with the details."

"I'm giving you all half an hour," Tony said. "She's going to bed after that and getting a good night's sleep."

A half hour went by, then Tony, true to his word, said, "Enough," which almost brought tears to Maggie's eyes. A lot of people helped take care of her, but it was about the details in her life, not her personally. It had been a long time since anyone had told her it was time to go to bed, but she was grateful he was stepping in for the moment, taking charge, even if he was only playing a role. She was too tired and emotionally wrung-out to think clearly.

Everyone stood. Garnet obviously was annoyed, but Maggie didn't understand why. Maybe she thought she could talk Maggie out of the marriage or something. Of course, Garnet's income also depended on Maggie continuing to do well, but Maggie believed her fans wouldn't criti-cize her in the end, not once they heard the whole story, such as it was, such as Tony had created, making himself a bit of a villain, after all, going after an engaged woman. A bad-boy image wouldn't hurt him in women's eyes.

"I'll be back in a few," he said quietly to her. "Dino and I are going to have a discussion."

"I can't lose him," she whispered back. "Once you and I end the marriage, I'm going to need him, you know."

Tony gave her an unfathomable look. "I admire loyalty, Margaret. He'll still be at your beck and call. Are you done memorizing your lines?"

"For tonight. I'll get up early tomorrow. I'm too tired to do more now."

"Why don't you get ready for bed, then. I won't be long."

He won't be long? What did that mean? That he would come back to say good-night? That he was going to join her?

That wasn't even an option, right?

Leesa was the only person left in the suite.

"You okay?" Maggie asked.

She sighed. "Mags, I know you want me kept in the dark for a reason, but I'm pretty sure I have the situation all figured out. You don't want to confide, okay, but don't ignore me."

Maggie saw hurt in her friend's eyes. She hugged her. "I'm so sorry. It's not my intention to ignore you. It's just that I'm not really in control of my life at the moment. I need you as much as ever. It'll all settle down again soon, I promise."

Leesa sniffed. "Thanks. I feel better."

"Good. Now how do you feel about cowboys?"

"They're probably fun to ride." She grinned. "You could verify that for me."

"I could, but I won't. Here's the thing. You and I will be moving to Tony's ranch tomorrow, so you'll need to pack up at some point during the day."

"Sure thing. What will you want to wear for the press conference?"

"Let's go take a look at the options." They headed into the bedroom, opened the closet doors. Her decision took no time at all. There was only one outfit that made the grade. "My red Western shirt, jeans and boots."

"Need me to go buy you a Stetson or something?" Her eyes sparkled.

"You know, that's not a bad idea. See if you can get a variety delivered to the set tomorrow. Or maybe Resistols are the in thing. Hmm. Just get an assortment, okay?"

Leesa nodded, looking even more amused.

"I know, I know," Maggie said. "Talk about life changes."

"Yep. I don't want to hear a word about hat hair," Leesa said with a laugh. "And I think I'd better get out of here before the man of the house comes back and sees me keeping you from your rest." She hugged her old friend. "Night. Thanks for keeping my life interesting."

The man of the house. Tony had easily assumed that role within the span of an hour. Maggie sensed they would knock heads now and then, each of them used to making their own decisions.

She grabbed a nightgown—mint-green, thigh length, silky but not transparent—and headed into the bathroom to get ready for bed. By the time she emerged, Tony was lounging in a chair by the bed, flipping through a fashion magazine he'd snagged from her bedside table.

"Figured you'd be in bed by now," he said, putting aside the magazine, but otherwise not moving.

"Leesa and I had to choose my clothes for the press conference." As casually as possible she walked across the room, folded back the quilt and climbed between the sheets. She shoved a couple of pillows against the headboard and settled against them. "Did you and Dino come to terms?"

"We did."

"And he'll be moving into your house, too?"

"He's renting an RV and will stay in it, next to the house." Tony stood. "Before you get all huffy about it, let me say that was his choice. I offered him a room inside. The rest of your security team will sleep in the bunkhouse.

Dino convinced me I was better off keeping them than hiring my own. I'm bowing to his expertise."

She was glad to see he could be flexible. "That sounds great, all of it. Thank you. And thank you for taking the heat regarding this relationship, Tony. That was incredibly generous of you."

"I'm not the one with a reputation to ruin." He started to unbutton his shirt.

"What are you doing?"

"Getting ready for bed." He continued undressing, pulling off his shirt and setting it aside neatly. Tugging off his boots. Then his fingers touched the metal button at his waist. It popped open. He slid the zipper down. Fascinated, she watched him. The jeans came down and were laid over a chair as neatly as his shirt.

Wearing his briefs, he joined her under the covers. "You didn't think I would leave my fiancée on her own, did you?" he asked, propped on an arm, facing her.

She wondered what he was thinking, but he was not an open book. When they'd talked about whether the marriage would include sex, just the idea of sharing his bed had her anticipating, but the marriage would be enough of a sham on its own. Adding to it by having sex as if they were a normal married couple would be leading him on—and for her it would be much harder to leave when it was time. A couple of months? She could manage that.

But now that he'd climbed into bed with her…

"I didn't know what your plans were," she said, finally answering his question. "I think you like to keep me guessing."

He smiled. It so transformed his face she could only stare. She definitely needed to make him smile more. He was a rugged-looking man, but his smile softened him. Then it went away as fast as it had come.

"Why'd you leave this morning without telling me goodbye, Margaret?"

"Because you would've stopped me, and I had lines to learn, and I needed to return the car I borrowed, and…"

"And?"

"I was afraid I'd get attached, afraid I'd let you take care of me. I need to take care of myself. Plus, I didn't want you to get caught with me—for your sake, not mine."

He stared at her for the longest time, then reached for her, pulling her close, tucking her head in that soothing, exciting spot between his neck and shoulder, her face almost touching his chest. "Don't do it again, okay?" he said into her hair. "Always tell me goodbye."

"Okay." What was he up to? Why was he holding her so close when nothing could come of it?

He held her a little tighter, kissed her forehead and said, "Sleep, darlin'. Just sleep."

It didn't take more than that. She closed her eyes and followed orders.

It'd been a long time since Tony had held a woman all night. For a little while after sex, yeah, but not the whole night. He tried to keep his hands from roaming over Maggie, but her nightgown was even softer than her skin, and every time he rubbed his hands up and down her back, she snuggled closer to him.

He could feel her breath, warm against his chest, her hand resting along his sternum. Her hair smelled of oranges, his favorite fruit. Her knee slipped between his thighs, bringing their bodies even closer. Sweat beaded his forehead. He'd already endured her proximity for several hours, with several more to go. If only he could fall asleep…

The next thing he knew, it was five o'clock. She'd rolled over, her very fine rear end pushed against him. He was fully, painfully aroused.

To distract himself, he made a mental list of what he needed to do this morning. Tell his parents his news before they heard it from someone else. Tell his housekeeper to get things ready at the house. Next week it would be time to move the herd. He always went along on the three-day chore each month, but this time? Maybe he'd have to hire an extra hand. He didn't want to leave Maggie alone, not with the security issues, no matter how competent Dino might be.

Maggie had been right about him. Dino was there to stay. He knew what it took to keep Maggie safe. Since that was the goal of both men, Tony left him in charge of her security, although Tony would take an active role. It was his ranch, after all, and his…fiancée.

"So, is that your championship buckle you're wearing or are you just happy to see me?" she asked, her voice sleepy. She wriggled closer.

"Hussy."

She went rigid. "I'm sorry," she said in a rush, moving away from him, obviously embarrassed at her unguarded response before she came fully awake.

He decided not to push his luck. For now he would be sleeping next to a woman who turned him on like no one else. A man could get used to that.

She hopped out of bed and headed to the bathroom. "I've got to get going," she said. "Lines to learn."

She shut the door. He tucked his hands behind his head and stared at the ceiling. He would be crazy to get used to having her there. She was only going to be around a few months at the most. In fact, she probably had another movie to do right after this one. He should ask about her schedule. But he couldn't traipse around the world, following her, being a stage husband, a lapdog—not even for show. He had a ranch to run, and his own self-respect to consider.

For sure a woman like her wouldn't settle for living in a place like his, either, isolated from the world.

He had to be very careful in his wooing. He was looking for more of what he'd had in the motel room—hot, wild sex with a beautiful woman—not permanence. They were oil and water. He'd done that once before on a much smaller scale. It hadn't worked then.

This time, he knew better than to try.

Chapter Six

Sue-Ellen Young, Tony's vibrant, seventy-two-year-old mother of four and grandmother of nine, wasn't often at a loss for words, but she hadn't uttered a sound since her youngest son told her later that morning that he was engaged to be married.

"To Maggie McShane?" she repeated eventually. She and Tony were sitting at the kitchen table, the same one he'd eaten at for the first eighteen years of his life.

"That's the one."

"The movie star." Awe and disbelief mingled in her voice.

He knew how she felt. "I don't know why you're questioning it. You saw our picture online."

"You told me it was an accidental kind of thing. Right place, right time, is what you said, and someone snapped a photo."

"And you were ticked at me for not getting her autograph. Now you can ask her yourself."

"Ask her…? As if I'd asked my own—oh, my stars, Maggie McShane is going to be my daughter-in-law. Fancy that. Well, when are you bringing her home to meet everyone? We'll throw a barbecue. How many people should I invite?" She pushed back from the table, grabbed a tablet of paper.

"Mom."

"Hmm?"

"A small affair the first time, okay? Just family. I'll have to let you know what works out, timewise. I don't know her schedule yet."

"Did you tell your father?"

"You're the first." As he'd driven in, Tony had seen his father in the round pen, but hadn't stopped to talk. He wanted to tell someone who would be happy for him first.

"You'll talk to him before you leave, right?"

Tony shrugged. "If he's available, I guess."

"He'll be thrilled."

"Maybe."

She gave him an admonishing look. "You're forty years old, and you can't see past when you were eighteen when it comes to him."

"He doesn't do anything to change that, either, Mom." Maybe his getting married would make a difference in his relationship with his father, maybe not. At the least, Hoyt Young might look at his son differently.

Of course, even that was ultimately an issue. He would be marrying her, but the marriage would be legal and fake at the same time. Maybe he'd end up looking worse in his father's eyes when the marriage ended. He hadn't considered that…

"Son?"

"Yeah, Mom?"

She patted his hand. "It's a good starting-over time, don't you think? New bride, the beginning of a new stage of your life. Making amends with your dad would be grand."

All Tony wanted from his father was respect for what he'd done with his life. Just because Tony had chosen a different path from his brothers—had been different all his life—shouldn't make him less in his father's eyes, but it always had. Especially regarding his rodeoing. Hoyt had never believed him, and wanted Tony to stay home and be part of the family business. He'd never understood his youngest son's need to do it his own way.

"I've got a ton of things to do," Tony said, standing. "There'll be a press conference late this afternoon, so you'll probably start getting phone calls."

"And what am I supposed to tell people about how you met? She was engaged, last everyone knew."

"You sure do keep up with Hollywood gossip."

"I made it a point after I saw you'd been kissing her. What mother wouldn't?"

"We met, I wanted her, so I went after her. The engagement was already ended—it just wasn't public knowledge yet. Beyond that, no one needs to know. It's our business, Maggie's and mine."

"You always were one to keep your own counsel."

"It's served me well, too." He bent down and kissed her cheek. "I'll give you a call later about the barbecue."

"Can I start telling people?"

"If you can stand it, would you wait until after the press conference? It won't be broadcast live or anything like that, so you'll still get to surprise people. I don't think

Maggie'd like the word out before she gives her statement. Her publicist is gonna stop by sometime today and give you advice about handlin' the press. Name's Garnet."

"Publicist? Seems like an awful lot of trouble for one little engagement."

"Little?" he repeated.

"Well, okay. I guess it won't be so little." She followed him to the kitchen door. "You sure she's gonna adapt to living where the mesquite's your nearest neighbor? Oh! Maybe you're giving up the ranch?"

"We have decisions to make, but I can assure you I'm not selling the ranch."

"She must have a fancy home in California. Or some highfalutin penthouse in New York City?"

He realized how little he knew about her. He'd better start getting a stronger sense of her and her life or he'd seem like an idiot. "I'll call you," he said to his mother, then left the house. He spotted his father still working in the round pen, his brothers draped on the fence, watching. Tony studied the man who'd sired him, a still-tall-and-sturdy cattleman of seventy-four hardworking years. He'd never been east of the Mississippi but had a lot to say about a world he knew little about except from what he saw on TV or read in the newspaper. *Opinionated* was Hoyt Young's middle name.

Tony shoved his hat down a little tighter and headed toward the pen. How many times as a boy had he clung to the fence watching his father train a horse? "Watch and learn," he'd always said in response to Tony's constant questions. *Shut up, pay attention and don't whine*—Hoyt Young's Three Commandments. The words were branded in Tony's brain. He'd learned not to say too much to his mother, either, since she always relayed his complaints to his dad, which only earned Tony extra time mucking stalls or some other menial task. Not that he hadn't done every possible menial job in his day—wasn't any the worse for it, either—but being ordered to do extra had been annoying, when all he'd wanted was answers to his questions.

Hoyt climbed down from the quivering quarter horse and passed the reins to Tony's brother Grady, who started a cooldown walk with him. Tony unlatched the gate as his father approached.

"Son," Hoyt said, coming through then relatching the gate, his bowlegged gait giving him a bit of a lean, side to side.

"Dad."

"I understand you've been rubbin' elbows with celebrities."

"Just one. That's why I'm here." Tony hated that his gut clenched. It shouldn't be like that. If he ever had kids of his own, they wouldn't fear him. "I'm marrying Maggie McShane."

"When?"

That's it? When? That's the only reaction he was going to get? "End of the month. In San Francisco. We'll be flying up there together, all the family."

"Pretty close to weanin' time. Takin' the calves to market."

Like he wouldn't know that? He had a spread of his own. Not that his father had acknowledged the success of the Lucky Hand. Just because his brothers had built houses on the family property and worked it—

Tony let it go. Old argument, old hurts. "You've never been to San Francisco, have you? Could be fun."

"Your mother's been houndin' me for years about goin'."

"Maybe you two could stay on a few extra days. Have a second honeymoon."

"Did you plant that idea in her head?"

"Nope. She'd see it as pretty romantic, though, if you suggested it."

Hoyt grunted.

They'd been walking toward Tony's truck and now came up beside it. "Well," Tony said. "Guess I'll be going. Mom's putting together a barbecue to meet Maggie."

"Sounds fine."

So. No congratulations. No questions. No slap on the back. No interest, apparently. Tony climbed into his truck. "So long."

A nod sufficed as answer, then his father turned around and ambled away. Tony shoved the truck in gear and drove off, his need for acknowledgment swept up with the trail of dust his truck left behind.

It was enough to choke a man.

Maggie peeked through the curtains as a crowd gathered in front of the old homestead on the movie set. Every cast and crew member was in attendance, their conversation and laughter drifting through the window glass. Television crews and journalists were checking sound and lights. A bunch of photographers claimed space near the front porch. She even spotted someone from *Meteor*, the gossip magazine that had suggested Maggie was pregnant with twins, hence the hurried-up wedding plans with Scott. Maggie blew a raspberry toward the jerk.

Leesa laughed from behind her. "Glad to see you're not intimidated by the crowd."

"It was nice of Mac to let us hold the press conference here."

"I imagine the publicity won't hurt when the movie

comes out. Press'll tap into it again when it's released. A remember-when? kind of thing."

And my marriage will be over by then. The thought stung her. "Still, Mac didn't have to make it easy for me, either. But this way, when Tony and I are done, we can just slip back inside the house until everyone leaves—or is chased off. Tony's here, right?"

She stepped away from the window and faced her assistant. She didn't want to admit to being worried he wouldn't show, that he'd changed his mind. He'd given his word, which meant she shouldn't worry, but she wasn't that confident yet.

"He's here. He said he'll join you in a few minutes. He's hanging with Dino, getting the lay of the land. Did you decide on a hat?"

"I'm going to ask Tony. He'll know." Maggie hadn't brought along her stylist, who would've known what looked the best on Maggie but not what was right. She wanted to fit in, for Tony to be proud to present her to his world. His parents would undoubtedly see bits and pieces of the conference, after the fact. "Garnet's got the statement?"

"In hand. She's mingling."

Boot steps sounded just before Tony swept into the living room from the back side of the house. He looked like a successful rancher in his black Western-cut suit, white shirt and bolo tie. Black hat in hand, he moved toward Maggie. She noticed he hadn't gotten a haircut and was glad. She loved the curls that touched his neck below his hat.

"I…I'll go," Leesa said. "Garnet will come get you when it's time."

"Garnet can park herself outside," Tony said, his gaze not straying from Maggie's. "I'll open the door when we're ready. She'd better be there."

"I'll tell her."

Maggie smiled at his take-charge attitude, especially since no one ever told Garnet what to do and got away with it.

"I'm thinkin' I should lock the door if I want to keep Garnet and her fury out," Tony said, a twinkle in his eye.

"You're a quick study."

He turned the lock, set his hat aside and closed the gap between them. "You look beautiful, Margaret."

She'd heard those words so many times they barely had impact anymore, yet her heart lurched when he said them, especially with him calling her Margaret—something no one else on the planet did. It was special, just between them. "Thank you. I need you to help me choose a hat to wear." She pointed to the assortment on the sofa.

He eyed them, leaned around her, grabbed one and handed it to her. "Don't wear it, though. Just carry it until you're done talking to the press. That'll signal the end. Plus, I expect you don't want your hair messed up."

Though she'd least expected it, he'd chosen the hat she liked the most, a low-brim, black wool one, with little adornment. She had no idea which brand it was.

"I'm kinda surprised you're wearing that outfit," he said. "That's the one we were photographed in. I didn't know a star wore the same outfit twice."

"This has sentimental meaning to me." She tugged on his bolo strings. "You look handsome."

"Thank you kindly."

"Are you nervous?" she asked.

"I did my share of interviews in my rodeo days." He put a finger to her chin, lifting it. "*You* look a little nervous, though. I figure a kiss'd take care of that, except your lips look ready for your close-up."

How could she keep resisting him if he kept saying things like that? And following through? His kisses made her weak.

She pointed to his belt buckle. "Did you win this one?"

"Nope. My prizewinners are in a case at home. This one's custom, my brand. And speaking of brands…" He held up his hand. A small, square velvet box sat in his palm.

An engagement ring? What else could it be? What a sweetheart of a man. "You didn't have to do that."

"Course I did." He pushed a tiny button. The lid popped open. Inside was a substantial square diamond set in a simple platinum band. "Jeweler called it an Asscher cut." He took out the ring and slid it on her finger.

Maggie didn't know what to say. How could he afford it? She couldn't ask, knew he wouldn't appreciate her questioning his ability to pay for it or offering to reimburse him. He was the one doing her a favor.

"It's exquisite," she said, aware he was waiting for a response. But "exquisite" didn't begin to describe it. It was flawless in her eyes.

"Looks like it fits okay."

"It fits perfectly. Tony." She flattened her hands on his chest. "You can return it, right? You made a deal with the jeweler to do that?"

A beat passed. "Course. He's a good friend of mine."

He'd hesitated just long enough to make her wonder if he was telling the truth.

"Well, darlin', what do you say we go feed ourselves to the wolves?"

She slipped her hand in his. "I still can't believe you're doing this for me. I don't know anyone else who would. Not anyone I could trust to keep it all a secret."

"No more thanks from you. It's a fair deal in my mind."

He tugged on her hand, walked her to the door and opened it. Lights flashed, people jostled, a sea of bodies crowding and shifting. Voices clamored.

Garnet, her back to the scene, gave Tony an I'll-deal-with-you-later look then she turned and addressed the audience.

"Good afternoon," she said into the bouquet of microphones in front of her. "What we've got here, folks, is a story better than any screenwriter could've conjured up…"

Chapter Seven

"I hadn't been paying attention before. Is all this property yours?" Maggie asked as they drove to Tony's house later. Her tension was ebbing by the minute. She was happy to be in the truck, alone with him, away from the crowd. She'd almost forgotten the traffic jams of home. Here, the wide-open spaces and far-off mountains mesmerized.

"I own forty acres, and I lease seventy thousand acres of public land for grazing. We'll take a ride on your first free day, and I'll show you. Or maybe you don't ride?"

"I do, although I've never ridden in country like this. I'm just a trail rider." She'd taken extra lessons before filming started, wanting to keep her role realistic.

"We've got trails," Tony said. "We're even starting a business to go along with it, but I'll tell you about that later. We figure to be up and running by next summer."

"Tourist trade?"

"Aimed at tourists, of course, and we want to make money at it, but we want people to see the land. To appreciate it. How many times will most folks ride a horse in their lives? We aim to have a cookout, too, where the guests and the cowboys can mingle."

"Dispel the myths that most people have?" she asked.

"That. And just let people have an appreciation for the cowboy life and why it should continue. You know, it's faster rounding up a herd with the help of a helicopter, but it takes jobs away from good men. There *is* a romance to it all, I think. I want it to continue."

"I really admire you, Tony."

He shrugged. "I'm just doin' my job."

It was much more than that, but she let it go for now. "How is it you've been able to spend so much time with me? I've always figured a cattleman to be one busy guy."

"Depends. We have two consistently busy times during the year—the spring castrating and branding, and the fall weaning and shipping the calves to market. Monthly, it takes us three days to move the herd to the next pasture, then there's twenty-seven days of other chores to do. Lots of fence work, stringing or repairing. It's feast or famine. And with the trail-ride business we've got going, we've always got something new to build."

"Your life has changed drastically with me around, especially with all of us moving to your property."

"Yep. Nothing else to do about it, however. It is what it is. You come with *people*."

"Most men—"

"Margaret," he interrupted. "Let's not go there. I'm not most men."

Which was one of the biggest understatements ever.

"You're right. Okay, I'll just say you did a great job with the press."

"Did I look appropriately sweet on you?"

She smiled. Oh, yeah. He'd played the role well, keeping her hand in his, looking at her adoringly. "*I* even bought it."

"I don't think Garnet's too pleased with me."

"That's her problem, and she'll either recover or quit." He sent a quick look in Maggie's direction. "Would she? Quit, I mean?"

"She's used to being in charge." And Tony hadn't let her be in charge.

"There can only be one Alpha dog in a pack," he drawled.

Maggie laughed. "And that's you, I take it."

"Well, sure. At least I got her to promise she would run everything past *me* as well as you before taking any information to the press. I know she's more skilled in that particular area than I am, but we need one common source if we're going to work as a team. I don't take orders well, in case you hadn't noticed, but I do listen."

"I can learn from you. Sometimes I forget that I'm Garnet's boss, not the other way around, because she's so…*right* all the time. Doesn't allow for much discussion."

He eyed her. "You sure keep destroying my image of a Hollywood star."

"In what way?"

"You just seem…normal. Most of the time."

"It's the controversial ones who make the headlines, you know. I've never caused controversy. Believe it or not, I'm not a rarity. It's the publicity machines that end up fostering a lot of bad press—and those few celebrities who really are screwed up."

"Misperceptions abound. Same is true of cowboys."

She'd seen the truth of his words. "You're complex. I like that."

"So are you. Which I also like."

A building came into view, a house.

"Is that your new ranch house?" she asked, admiring the wood-sided structure, which spread out like she would've expected a ranch house would, with lots of windows facing an unparalleled view.

"Yep. The couple standing on the porch are Butch and Sadie Kelly, my foreman and housekeeper."

"Sadie? I don't think I've heard that name except in old Westerns. How did they come to work for you?"

"Butch and I rode rodeo together. He's my age. She's younger—and four months pregnant. We've been friends for a long time. Just seemed like a good thing, them working with me. Although once the trail-ride business gets going, she won't have time to help me out with the house, not with a baby to take care of, too. She's going to be fully involved in that business."

He stopped the car near the porch. Dino pulled up behind him in his rented RV/security command center. Leesa followed in the SUV they'd been using since their arrival.

Tony introduced everyone. Dino left to move the RV alongside the house. Leesa and Butch took suitcases and garment bags inside.

"We just saw your press conference on YouTube," Sadie said, excitement bubbling from her. "I never noticed before, Tony, but you kinda look like John Wayne!"

"See?" Maggie said to Tony, and feeling an instant bond with Sadie. "I'm glad I'm not the only one to recognize that."

"Aw, shucks, ma'am," Tony said, tipping his hat, a slight smile softening his face.

Sadie rolled her eyes. "How soon would you like to have dinner, Ms. McShane? Tony said to make something simple, so I fixed Cobb salad."

"Oh, that sounds perfect. I'm starving. And please call me Maggie."

"I will, thank you. You'll probably want to freshen up first. Maybe have a drink and relax?" Sadie asked.

"Iced tea, if you have it, thanks." She wondered what Tony was thinking. He'd been pretty quiet most of the time since the press conference, answering her questions but not really keeping a conversation going. "May I have a tour of the house first?" she asked Tony.

He hesitated. "Would you mind if Sadie takes you around? I've got a couple of things to check on before it gets dark."

"No problem."

"Okay. See you in a little bit." He went down the stairs and walked away, heading toward the side of the house—and Dino's RV.

"I've never seen him look happier," Sadie said.

"How can you tell? He hardly ever smiles."

"It's inside him. I can see it." Sadie's eyes sparkled. "Who would've ever thought it? Tony and you. You are a very lucky woman."

Most people would've said that Tony was a lucky man. Maggie was so happy that Sadie saw it differently—because Maggie did feel lucky. "I think so, too."

"Ready to see the house?"

Maggie fell in step beside her. "Tony tells me you're four months pregnant."

Sadie's hand slid across her abdomen. "We'd been trying for five years, so this is extra special."

It was one of the biggest reasons why Maggie had wanted to marry Scott—he'd wanted children, too, right away. Or so he'd said. She'd begun to wonder a lot about that relationship now, after the fact, even her own motivations. She'd wanted a family to replace the one that was gone. But the speed at which the relationship happened, then the fact he hadn't made a lot of time for her, gave her pause now. Granted, he'd been filming, but he hadn't invited her to join him, even when she'd had a few days free to do so.

Had it all been a publicity stunt for him, and she'd fallen for it because she so desperately wanted a family? Had he told her what she wanted to hear rather than the truth? It seemed possible, now that she could take an unbiased look at the situation. He could've been using her to further his career. And her being named the villain in the public's eye about the breakup wouldn't hurt him, either.

Maggie followed Sadie into a large, open living room, with a stone fireplace, rustic but comfortable-looking furnishings, a large area rug atop wood floors, a masculine, Western feel. "I understand this was recently built."

"He moved in about six months ago. Butch and I have a double-wide across the yard, but after the movie's done, Tony's going to remodel the old homestead for us. It's spacious and closer to the corrals."

Maggie's cell phone rang. She looked at the screen—Scott. "I'm sorry. I need to take this call."

Sadie pointed. "Tony's office. You can shut the door."

"Thanks." She said hello as she walked.

"Just wanted to let you know that my part's done," he said.

"I'll bet you got a lot of sympathy."

He chuckled. "Yeah. I still don't know why you decided to let me off the hook instead of being the one who done you wrong, since that's what I was."

The sound of his voice grated. She was glad it was the end for them. "Doesn't really matter, does it? It worked out for you. How long until you go public with Gennifer?"

"I don't know. Not too long."

"There were rumors about your affair with her even before you broke it off with me. People may draw their own conclusion about what really happened. The truth could come out."

"Unless you or I set the record straight, it'll only be speculation, though. I'll keep my mouth shut."

"So will I." She wasn't sure about Gennifer, however, and Maggie didn't want the truth to come out. She wanted it over with.

"I know, Maggie. That's one thing I can take to the bank."

"I wish I could say the same about you, Scotty."

A couple of beats passed. "I'm sorry you don't trust me."

"Me, too. But you were right about something. I *am* glad it's over between us. Tony's been really good to me."

"Yeah, well, he's got America's Sweetheart, doesn't he? That's major bragging rights. If you think being engaged to you upped *my* value, think what it does for a cowboy."

Annoyed, Maggie said goodbye and shut her phone. She settled into the big leather chair behind Tony's desk. Scott was wrong. Tony wasn't dazzled by her. He hadn't been blinded by her star status at all. He'd been chivalrous and kind. He had a strong sense of himself and his own needs, wasn't relying on her to build up his ego. She liked that about him, liked that she couldn't push him around, or get him to do something he wasn't comfortable with.

A knock had her sitting up straight. The door opened. Tony stuck his head inside.

"Everything okay?" he asked.

She climbed out of the chair, went up and hugged him, even if it wasn't what she should be doing. She didn't want him to misinterpret. She would keep her word not to make love with him. She just needed a hug. "Everything is wonderful."

He slipped his arms around her. She closed her eyes and breathed him. "Everything okay with you?" she asked.

"Yes."

Not *yep* but a much more serious answer—yes. It comforted her. She had to make sure she didn't mess up their chances for taking a deep friendship out of this relationship when it ended, the only way to keep this special man in her life. He'd already become that important.

Tony propped his pillows against his headboard and took in the master bedroom, wondering what Maggie thought of it. It was a good-size room—he needed space—but it was probably small compared to her own. Would he see where she lived before they called it quits? He'd like to.

At the moment, she was in the attached bathroom getting ready for bed. The sound of water reached him now and then, but the door was shut, so he couldn't watch her. He had no hope that would ever change, but he'd like it to.

It stunned him to think they'd known each other only two days. Two days. And yet they were getting married. Crazy.

He tucked his hands behind his head. He was tired, yet thoughts were running through his head like a herd spooked by a mountain lion. The security issues wore him out. In the end he'd been grateful for Dino's expertise.

They had the same goals, after all, but it was a whole new world to Tony.

His bedroom blinds were down. That was new, too. Dino didn't like that Tony's house had few window coverings. For the most part, there hadn't been any need for them, as isolated as the ranch was. There were blinds in the bedrooms that were hardly ever let down, but the living room, dining room and kitchen windows were naked—which meant anyone with a supertelephoto lens could take pictures from far-off.

Tony had taken Dino out in the Jeep to check for probable observation-danger spots, then they set up a plan to keep those areas under constant surveillance when Maggie was home.

Finally the bathroom door opened and she came out. Her scent hit him first, light and arousing. She wore a T-shirt of his, something he guessed she thought wouldn't be sexy to him. Did she really expect him to keep his hands off her when she was wearing something he could slip off her in a wink?

He folded back the sheet, welcoming her. He'd turned off all the lights but one, a bedside lamp, more for mood than reading.

"You smell *female,*" he said as she slipped in bed beside him.

"It's just lotion."

"I think it's just you."

"You're a very sweet man."

That caught him off guard. "No, I'm not, and don't go thinking that. You've known me all of two days."

Maggie looked him in the eye. "I know that Sadie adores you, and I think she's an excellent judge of character. I've learned that Dino respects you, and I *know* he's an excellent judge of character. Yes, we have a lot to learn about each other, but I already figure you can handle yourself just fine in a fight, at the poker table or throwing a rope over a steer. None of that changes the fact you are also very sweet."

Well, no one had ever called him that before, not to his face. A man was made on his reputation. He liked being thought of as hard. Saved a lot of battles along the way. "Don't go spreading that rumor around," he said, then heard her laugh softly, which relaxed him. He hadn't expected to be relaxed, being in the same bed with her without being allowed to touch.

"What's your schedule like?" he asked. "How much longer will you be working on this film? And what comes after it?"

"We started off in L.A. on a soundstage. We're supposed to finish up here a week before the wedding. After that I have a month off, then I'm off to New York. I signed on to do a little independent film for a friend. It'll be a pretty good departure for me, except I hope the fact I've been playing a certain kind of role forever doesn't hurt his film."

"Why would it?"

"If the audience doesn't believe me in this different role, they might not buy into the movie."

He guessed he could understand that, but it sure showed how narrow-minded folks could be. "After that?"

"I've signed on for another feature, but I've got a lot of downtime in between projects. I've been working since I was five, you know. I made a conscious decision to slow down a little, separate myself some."

"Why?"

"Preparing for the future. I'd like to do something different—hence the indie film. But I'd been planning on marriage and babies, too."

Babies?

"Don't panic," she said, meeting his gaze. "I don't mean with you. It was a dream, that's all. I'm on the pill. I'll stay on the pill. No surprises, I promise."

"Okay. Where do you live?"

"I have a home on the coast in California, near Malibu, and a co-op in New York City." She settled into her pillow, pulling the sheet to her shoulders.

"Which do you like most?"

"Neither. Both."

He could hear her smile.

"Two different houses, two entirely different ways of life," she said. "Your home is beautiful, by the way. I didn't get a chance to tell you earlier. It's everything I imagined a house of yours would be."

"How'd you turn out so normal?"

"Am I?" She laughed. "First, my parents, I guess, who made sure I lived as normal a life as possible, for a child actor. Then when they and my little brother died in a car accident when I was ten, my grandparents took over. My grandmother could've led an army. There was no disobeying her, ever. And yet I always felt loved." She went quiet for a moment. "She instilled in me the importance of being real, of not buying into all of the hype about myself. I could've easily gone the way of a lot of other child stars, but she wouldn't have let me."

"I think you probably had something to do with that yourself. You made your own choices, good ones, apparently," he said, his admiration of her notching even higher. He picked up a strand of her hair, moving it back from her face, letting him see her better. "Most kids rebel. It's the nature of the beast. You didn't seem to. You've never done a nude scene, according to my research."

"You researched me?"

"Well, Margaret, I'm going to marry you, aren't I? Figured I should know a little about what I'm getting into."

"And you believe everything you read about me online?"

"Course not. But it puts questions to ask in my head. So, how come you've always kept your clothes on?"

"I always pictured my grandparents seeing me. It was a horrifying image. Anyway, I had my rebellious moments. I just never got caught—and they weren't huge. Frankly I've been too busy working to have much of a life outside it." She smiled. "I'm tired."

I'm tired. The words were an age-old, universal signal of disinterest. And since she believed he'd agreed to no sex, she had faith she could just lie in bed with him and sleep.

Okay. Maybe this first night, he could do that. He needed to seduce her, and seduction should start outside the bedroom.

He almost laughed out loud at the idea. Hell, they'd already made love. Twice. It probably wouldn't take much to change her mind…

Then he saw she'd closed her eyes.

Dilemma solved. For tonight, anyway.

Maggie knew how to fake being asleep. It was an important skill for an actor. She could keep her eyes from moving, and her breaths measured. After a while, Tony's body relaxed. He was asleep.

She'd pretended to fall asleep midconversation because she had a sense things were going to get tense between them. He hadn't done anything but move her hair from her face, but it was the tender way he'd done it.

She didn't understand. She thought he believed as she did, that sex would only complicate things. And no birth control except abstinence was a hundred percent. If she ended up pregnant, he wouldn't let her go. She wouldn't want to go.

So, it was better to leave it like this. It was hard to share a bed with him, knowing he was less than a foot away, and he offered comfort and excitement and pleasure. But it would be harder still to end a marriage after even more intimacy. She already knew how great that intimacy could be.

All in all, it was proving to be the biggest test of fortitude she'd ever endured.

She hoped she passed.

Chapter Eight

Nerves had Maggie rubbing her hands along her thighs and staring out the window of Tony's pickup a few days later, headed to a command performance. Time to meet the family.

"You got lucky," she said, eyeing the landscape, hard but incredibly beautiful. She could pick out the mesquites now, at least, if not the other varieties of flora.

"How's that?"

"I have no family for you to meet."

"Right," he said dryly. "Just a legion of fans, fellow celebrities and every kind of journalist there is. That's so equitable."

She laughed. "You're handling it great." Admirably, in fact. "I could use a quick brushup on your family."

"Sure. Father, Hoyt, seventy-four, still working the ranch and training horses. Mother, Sue-Ellen, seventy-two, still running the house and a good part of the ranch. We had a big fiftieth-anniversary bash for them two years ago, even the governor came. I'm the baby of the family. Oldest brother, Cal, has three kids. Next is Grady, who has four. Then my sister, Mary Beth, who has two. She's four years older than me, so there's quite an age difference between us all. They're all married, I think happily."

"You think?"

"Everyone has some rocky times, don't they? I figure they'll all be on their best behavior today, meeting you."

"I know it's intimidating, but I hope I can put them at ease quickly."

"You'll know when they start insulting you that you've been accepted."

Great. She had to wait for that to know? She wished he hadn't told her. "Did they like your ex?"

"Nope."

She waited. "That's all you're going to say?"

"The marriage lasted less than one rodeo circuit. Not a lot *to* say."

"Why'd you marry her?"

"Because I was young and horny."

She laughed. "Why'd she marry you?"

"Same, I expect. I was an up-and-comer, too. She didn't have dreams of her own, so she tagged along on mine. That never works. She found herself someone with a bigger dream, and off she went."

"You're very matter-of-fact about it."

"Darlin', as I said before, it was a long time ago. I was just a kid."

"And since then you haven't been tempted to marry?" She'd been wondering about his past. He hadn't been forthcoming.

"Not even close."

"Haven't lived with anyone?"

"I've had overnighters, Margaret. I haven't been in love, if that's what you're circling around."

He'd seen through her. He was a great catch, so she really didn't understand why he was still single. "Can't I be curious about you?"

"Course you can. I'm answering your questions, aren't I?"

"Short and to the point."

"Is there another way?" He gave her a probing look.

"Yes, long and expansive."

"Isn't my style."

She sighed. "I know. Tell me about the family ranch."

"My grandfather started it, but my dad took it places, made it successful. Cal and Grady were happy to stay on and work it with him, so they built houses on the property. My sister lives in Scottsdale with her stockbroker husband. She never cared much about ranching."

"Why did you go off on your own?"

"'Cause my dad and I butt heads all the time. He didn't want me to go rodeoing. I couldn't wait to go. I loved the land, I loved the work, but I couldn't live with him one more minute, especially once my brothers and sister weren't living in the house anymore and there wasn't a buffer between me and Dad, except Mom. Nothing I did pleased him. And I wanted to see something of the world before I settled down."

"Is he proud of you for what you've done?"

"He's never said so."

Since all she'd ever known from her parents and grandparents was pride and love, she couldn't imagine how Tony felt.

"Here we are."

Maggie saw a house not as new as Tony's, but not as ancient as the old homestead where they were filming. Scattered around the property were structures similar to the ones on Tony's property—a barn, large open storage shed, different kinds of animal pens, small and large.

"Looks like we're the first ones to arrive. Mom must've told the others to come a little later, give her some time to drill you."

She caught the twinkle in his eyes. "So, it's your mom I need to worry about, not your dad?"

"If Dad asks you more than one question, I'll be shocked. It's not his way. He'll listen to what you say, though. Don't think otherwise. He's paying attention even when he's not paying attention."

She blew out a long breath. "Okay." At least she was wearing her armor of boots, jeans and a new yellow shirt. Being dressed right for the occasion always helped.

Tony set his hand over hers, clenched in her lap. "Mom'll be nervous, too."

"Really?"

"Course. And if you're ever feeling uncomfortable, just give me a sign. I'll make an excuse to get you outside—or home, if you need that instead."

"What kind of sign?"

He stopped the truck beside the house and turned off the engine. "You choose."

"I'll tug on my right ear."

He slid an arm along the seat behind her, then tucked her hair behind her left ear. "And if you tug on this one instead? I wouldn't want to leave you stranded."

She shivered from his touch as he traced her ear with his fingertip. He hadn't touched her a lot the past few days, mostly only around other people to keep up the show, but he was good at it when he did. Knew exactly what places to caress and how soft to do it. She'd been aroused several times each day just looking at him, then the slightest touch had her yearning.

"Okay, then. If I tug on *either* ear," she said.

He nuzzled her, his lips brushing the tender skin below her ear. "Works for me. And how about if you want to have your way with me, you just swivel your hips some. My old bedroom's still available."

Stunned, she laughed, but turned her head, was close enough to kiss him. What was going on with him? It wasn't like him at all. "You're crazy."

"But in a good way."

"The jury's still out on that."

He raised his brows. "Well, okay, then. I've been fed to your wolves. Let's go feed you to mine."

"You're not helping."

He laughed. The sound was so unexpected, she just stared.

"Sit still for a second," he said, "and I'll come around and open your door."

"You don't have to—"

"My mother's been watching us from the kitchen window. She tried to drill manners into me. I want her to know it worked."

So *that* was why he'd been seducing her. They were being observed.

"Except this is the first time you've done so," she said, disappointed that it had all been for show.

"Only because you've always just hopped out." He planted a kiss on her lips, short and sweet, like punctuation at the end of a sentence. Conversation over. Period.

She watched him amble around the truck and open her door. She wished she could take him up on the offer to use his bedroom. "Something smells incredible," she said instead.

"That would be my father's barbecued ribs, slow cooking out back."

"It's making my stomach growl."

"Wait'll you taste the fixin's. Mom makes the world's best cowboy beans and biscuits. There'll be cobbler of some kind, too. Probably peach."

"Do you think she'd get a bad impression of me if I just ask where the grub is when I meet her?"

"I think she'd get a kick out of it."

Maggie wouldn't do it, of course. She wanted to make a good impression, and getting overly casual at the beginning probably wasn't a good idea.

It struck her then that she'd never been taken to meet parents before. She'd never dated anyone long enough for that to happen. The thought shot her nerves into the stratosphere.

Fortunately Tony kept her hand in his as they went into the house. The living room was both similar to and different from Tony's—similar in its Western style but different in that a woman's touch was evident in the decorating—some nice touches, like flowers and candles. The art on the walls wasn't all Western in nature, either, but portraits, too, something lacking at Tony's place. But here there was family, and lots of it. Generations. Before she could ask Tony about them, his parents came into the room.

Hoyt Young was shorter than Tony by several inches, but still a tall, imposing man with a full head of salt-and-pepper hair. Tony had inherited his straight nose, strong jaw and broad shoulders, but his eyes were all Sue-Ellen, who came forward to embrace, and made Maggie feel like she was hugging her mother again.

Her throat burned; her eyes welled. She tried to blink the threatening tears back before the hug ended and she had to look the woman in the eye.

"Welcome to our home and our family," Sue-Ellen said as she released Maggie. Tall and slender like her husband, Sue-Ellen wore her gray hair short and casual, framing her delicate, lined face. Maggie could only wish for a complexion as beautiful at that age.

"Thank you so much," Maggie said, hoping her smile masked her bubbling emotions. "Your home is beautiful. Hello, Mr. Young," she said, looking at Tony's father.

He reached across to shake her hand. "You can call us by our given names, Hoyt and Sue-Ellen. Good to meet you."

Maggie felt Tony's hand come to rest on her shoulder. She leaned against him a little as his mother gestured toward a couple of large sofas. A tray of appetizers sat on a nearby coffee table. She took requests for drinks. Maggie offered to help and followed her into the kitchen. The room had been updated, obviously, since the appliances and countertop looked relatively new, but there was an old scarred kitchen table with six chairs around it. She ran her hand over the surface.

"Hoyt made me that table shortly after we were married," Sue-Ellen said, getting glasses from the cupboard for iced tea. "The kids did homework there. Played games. Put together puzzles on rainy days. Did all the craft stuff that kids do. It was a lot of fun when it was full every day. I miss the noise."

Maggie tried to picture it. She had few clear memories of her life with her parents and brother, just bits and pieces, much of it reconstructed from pictures and videos. Life with her grandparents had been quiet. "I never had that. I can see how fun it would be."

"Yes. Then one day you notice there's no one there anymore. It's hard. Then you get grandchildren, and it's better again. Would you mind grabbing a couple of beers for the men? They're in the fridge."

Grateful for something to do, Maggie went to the refrigerator.

"I know a lot about you because of the Internet, but not how much of it is real," Sue-Ellen said, as if testing the waters. "You're just as pretty in person, though. You and Tony fit well together."

Maggie understood what she meant. After watching the press coverage of their news conference, Maggie had thought that they looked like a couple. Sweet on each other, as Tony put it, and physically well matched.

"He's a very good man," Maggie said. "He gives a lot of credit to you for who he is."

"Does he? Well, isn't that sweet. I suppose he's told you he was cut from a different cloth from his siblings."

"He didn't put it that way," Maggie said carefully. She didn't want to offend anyone. "It sounds to me like he was just determined to choose his own path and didn't want help getting there. I admire him immensely."

Sue-Ellen nodded. She picked up the glasses of tea. "Let's get ourselves back in the living room so there'll be conversation in the house." She gave Maggie a quick smile.

The yearning that filled Maggie for family and home and stability skyrocketed. She wanted that more than anything. Then came the guilt that his parents were making an emotional investment in her as their son's wife-to-be.

When she and Tony split up, how would he explain it to his family? She didn't want them to think poorly of her, but she guessed she couldn't change that. Even if she tried not to get too close, it was going to hurt.

And knowing Tony as she was beginning to already, she knew he would be the one to take the public blame for the marriage ending. It wasn't fair. Maggie knew it wasn't fair. She'd have to figure out something so that he didn't come out the bad guy in the deal.

That thought stayed with Maggie all afternoon as more and more family came and filled up all the space. Several of Tony's nieces and nephews were in college and couldn't make it to the party. Most were high schoolers and so accustomed to each other, they took off after eating to go riding or hang out together in the barn. The initial awe that everyone displayed settled down soon enough as Maggie engaged them in conversation. Couldn't they see she was just as much in awe of all of them for what they had?

No one had insulted her yet, though. She was waiting for that. Acceptance. It was probably too soon to hope for it, however.

They all sat under a covered patio after the meal, the heat dragging them down, especially on top of the enormous meal. Maggie noticed that Tony got along reasonably well with his brothers, and his sister teased him like crazy. An occasional smile touched his lips, but mostly he just teased back, dryly, pointedly, until she reacted. The byplay fascinated Maggie. Her brother had been five when he died. They'd never had a chance to have a real sibling relationship, not like this.

"Look at those kids," Sue-Ellen said, looking out toward the range at six of her grandchildren, racing their horses and stirring up dust. "So grown up, all of 'em." She cast a glance at Tony and Maggie sitting together nearby. "It'll be fun to have little ones around again."

"Mother!" Tony's sister, Mary Beth, said, her expression apologetic as she looked at Maggie to see her reaction.

Sue-Ellen shrugged. "I'm just sayin'."

Maggie smiled then met Tony's gaze when she felt his fingers squeeze her shoulder. He tugged on his ear. She laughed. He tugged again. So, he wanted to make a break for it? Was he uncomfortable with the subject of babies? She wondered if he was serious. Was she supposed to make some kind of excuse and get them away? It wouldn't be right for her to do that. He needed to be the one—

"Yankin' your chain, darlin'," he said, leaning close to her.

"I was panicking, trying to figure out what to do," she whispered back.

"I could see that." He looked pleased that he'd gotten her all shook up like that.

"Just for that, I'm going to kiss you right here in front of your entire family." She paused, waiting for his reaction, but he didn't move away. His eyes challenged her. She inched closer and kissed him, lingering a couple of seconds, until hoots and hollers went up around them.

"See? Babies ahead," Sue-Ellen said, satisfied.

But Maggie began to wonder about his behavior in front of his family. Usually steady and self-confident, he'd hardly let her out of his sight all day. In fact there'd barely been a moment when he wasn't touching her, either holding her hand or slipping his arm around her, keeping her tethered to his side.

At first she thought he'd finally really relaxed, feeling at home, as if there was no chance of media intrusion to ruin things. But as the afternoon passed, she realized he was actually more tense than usual. He'd hidden it very well, but she was also coming to know him very well.

What would make him stake that kind of claim on her in front of his family?

"We've all heard about what movie stars demand in their dressing rooms," Mary Beth said. "Some of it sounds crazy. What do you have to have?"

"It's pretty boring, I think. Bottles of flavored iced tea, fresh fruit, cheese and crackers. I don't like to work on a really full stomach. Oh, and ice cream. I love ice cream."

"What flavor?" Mary Beth asked.

"Anything with chocolate or caramel in it."

"You don't look like you indulge in it."

"I work out. Hate it," she added, wrinkling her nose. "At home I have a trainer, because it's hard to get myself motivated otherwise. On set, it's difficult to find time, since we usually start very early in the morning with hair and makeup. Then there's a lot of hurry-up-and-wait going on."

The conversation about moviemaking went on for a while longer, with almost everyone asking something, especially when the kids came back and joined them.

"Maggie, can I ask you a personal question?" Mary Beth asked.

Whatever other conversations had been taking place came to a halt instantly. Maggie stopped herself from smiling. "Sure."

"After you announced the end of your engagement to Scott Gibson and your new engagement to Tony, there were a lot of comments that weren't really flattering about you. How did it make you feel?"

Tony frowned. "You don't—"

"No, it's fine," Maggie said. "I don't mind. I was okay with it, Mary Beth. *I* know my engagement to Scott was over before Tony and I got together. If people don't believe that, it's their problem."

"Didn't some of it hurt?"

"A little. I've lived my life honorably, I believe, so I can't say it didn't sting some. But I also know how the business works. If there's a chance to sell more magazines or get more viewers, they grab it." Plus, how could she object? It was only payback for the deception she and Tony were perpetrating. Garnet had pushed Maggie to do an interview on one of the reputable network magazine shows, but she'd turned it down, much to Garnet's consternation. When the marriage ended, she didn't want sound bites of herself extolling being in love and marrying such a wonderful man haunting her—or Tony. At least, no more than were already in the vaults.

"You just keep bein' honest," Hoyt said. "It's the right thing to do. And you know our family'll back you, right?"

Maggie felt Tony react. His father hadn't uttered a word directly to her since his first greeting when she arrived. She'd seen him speak to his wife and other sons, but short sentences, not having conversations. He'd come close to having a conversation with her just now. "Thank you so much," she said to him, her throat closing a little.

He nodded and sat back.

"Why, anyone can see you're an upright and truthful young woman," Sue-Ellen added, leaning over to pat Maggie's knee.

Guilt swamped Maggie. *How can I do this to them? How can Tony? I'm falling in love with his family.* They continued to bombard her with questions, but she kept a smile on her face.

She wasn't paid the big acting bucks for nothing.

Chapter Nine

"So, where it says here in the script, Grace and Marcus kiss, it means a full-on lip-lock?" Tony asked a few nights later. They'd retired to his bedroom right after dinner, as had become their habit. He'd been running lines with her for the past hour, had noticed that things were heating up between the two lead characters and came to his own conclusion before they'd even reached the page where the scene would end in a kiss.

Tapping a pen lightly against her chin, she didn't look up from her script. "It's make-believe, you know," she said, as if he'd lived in a cave all his life. "Anyway, it's just Rafe. No big deal."

No big deal? Rafe Valente was no big deal? He was certainly a big deal with women all around the world, as well-known for his play-the-field ways as Maggie was for her good-girl ways, probably one of the reasons they'd been paired together for the movie—built-in conflict just in the pairing.

Tony also knew that Maggie had been romantically linked to more than one of her leading men through the years.

When he didn't say anything, she finally gave him her full attention, even setting her script aside. "What's going on, Tony? You've been different ever since the barbecue at your parents' house. That's three days."

"Different how? And why aren't you answering my question?"

"Yes, it's a full-on lip-lock," she answered evenly. "How else do people kiss?"

"How long does it usually take to get it right? Till the director is okay with it?"

She smiled in a way he didn't like at all. "Why, Tony, I do believe you're jealous."

"Hell, no, I'm not jealous. I don't get jealous. Waste of time and energy, and destructive at that."

"I'm glad to hear it. It'd probably be a good idea for you to stay away from the set, though, just in case it does end up tapping into your time and energy." She went back to reviewing her dialogue, mouthing her lines, gesturing.

"I can handle it," he insisted.

"Good." She climbed off the bed and paced while she continued. She was working on an entire page of uninterrupted dialogue where her character was supposed to be explaining why she'd been lying to the hero about her reasons for showing up on his ranch, interrupting the man's ten years of self-enforced isolation.

"I've been different, how?" Tony pressed.

"Tony, I really need to get this done. I always show up prepared."

"This'll only take a minute. Quick answer and you're done."

She sighed, then she sat on the bed beside him, facing him. "Okay. You were different at your parents' house. You...stuck to me like glue, almost."

"I was looking out for you. First time meeting a big family like that can be nerve-racking."

"I think I was holding my own okay. And you *were* behaving differently, I don't care what you say. Were you afraid I'd embarrass you or something?"

"Hell, no. I was proud to have you on my arm." Maybe he shouldn't tell her that...

"It seemed beyond pride to me." She looked away for a second, as if debating something. "Were you feeling as bad as I was for misleading them? Before too long we'll be telling them the marriage is over—something we already know. And your mother is so happy. Was that weighing on you?"

Mostly he'd been showing off. He was going to be marrying Maggie McShane, the circumstances of which didn't matter, as far as he was concerned, and yet at the end of the party he hadn't been as satisfied as he'd thought he would be. His father hadn't treated him any differently, just like years ago when he'd won his first trophy—

Whoa. Now he was thinking of her as a trophy?

He took Maggie's hands in his. "Yes. I felt bad about lying to my family, too," he said, deciding to take the easy, and still honest, way out. He didn't want her to know how frustrated he was with his father—had been for years— because he'd never acknowledged what he'd accomplished. It was as if it was expected of him. And, unlike his brothers, he'd done it all without his father's help.

"That's the worst part of this whole situation, at least to

me," she said quietly. "Sometimes I would forget. They all made me feel so much at home. I'd thought they would be hard to get to know, based on some of the things you'd told me. I found them all very open."

Because you haven't disappointed them yet, he thought. Then they'll shut down. Oh, not completely. He was still part of the family, after all, but he wasn't treated the same as his brothers and sister, not by his father, anyway.

"Satisfied?" Maggie asked. "Did I answer your questions?"

"Yeah." He wanted to kiss her, hard and long, then drag her under him, and make her forget she would be kissing America's Heartthrob tomorrow. It was getting more and more difficult not to make love to her, not to hold her close during the night, although sometimes that happened spontaneously as they slept. Whether he instigated it or she did, he didn't know. He just knew that occasionally he woke up with her nestled against him, her hand on his abdomen, her breath warm against his flesh.

He needed to work harder at this wooing business, he decided. He'd been treading too carefully.

"I think we should practice the kiss," he said.

She smiled. "Really?"

He sat up a little more and met her gaze. "What do you think? Soft? Hard? Over and done with fast? Or slow and easy?" He framed her face with his hands, let his thumbs brush her cheeks, saw her eyes darken.

"The director will tell—"

He shook his head. "If you were the director. You know the script. How would you see it?" He wanted her to take the lead. She hadn't so far, not since that helluva night in bed they had at the motel. But he also thought she'd been holding back a lot. A whole lot. Her body language spoke volumes. "Pretend you're Marcus and I'm Grace," Tony said. "You lead."

Her eyes flashed. She liked the idea. The challenge. "I have to get on my knees," she said, moving to do so. "Be taller than you."

There was something strangely exhilarating about the reversal of their positions, of her looking down on him, especially when she lowered herself toward him. But as she neared, she grinned.

"Stay in character," he urged, the anticipation driving him crazy. His heart thundered.

Finally she kissed his temple, his eyebrow, his eyelid. He closed his eyes, letting himself just feel, enjoying her being in charge. She made a small sound of need as she repeated the kisses on the other side. She rubbed his earlobes with gentle fingers. When had they become erogenous zones? His throat vibrated.

She pulled back.

"Don't stop," he said, looking at her, seeing something like panic in her eyes.

"It's one thing for us to kiss in front of other people because we need to seem like a couple," she said. "This is…different. Tempting. Too tempting."

"We won't let it get out of hand."

"I'm not sure I trust myself that much."

Ahh. Just what he wanted to hear. "Then trust *me*. I won't let anything happen except a kiss. Keep going. It's safe."

She stared back, then finally, "Close your eyes."

He did. Her lips brushed across his, feathery touches that woke up every suppressed hormone in his body. She pulled back, came at him again, the contact lasting a little longer, a little deeper. Then her tongue traveled along his jaw, leaving a damp trail that her breath made even more sensitive. Her mouth descended again, her tongue lightly sweeping his lips. He opened them, let her inside, all warm and curious.

A long, throaty sound escaped him as he met her tongue with his. She pushed him back onto the bed, straddled him, made love with her tongue. He ran his hands down her back, over her rear and cupped her, spreading her legs farther apart, settling her on him, aligning her, feeling her heat even through their clothes.

He needed this. Needed her. He'd been slowly going crazy having her nearby for the past couple of weeks and not doing anything about it, except get stirred up when they were in public. He thought he had a lot of self-control—

She sat straight up, panting, pressed a hand to her mouth. "We can't do this."

He didn't say anything. How could he?

"It'd be too hard to end it when the time comes." She moved off him. "I'm sorry. I should've trusted my instincts." She went into the bathroom and shut the door.

And he was left frustrated, physically and mentally. A common state, these days.

He should stay away. Tony knew he should stay far, far away from the set. Maggie wasn't going to be happy that he'd shown up in time to watch her love scene, but he was going crazy at home, barking orders at his foreman, making his own horse skittish, feeling a need to do something physical and strenuous.

Instead he'd taken a drive to the set, parked way off in the distance as he'd been told to and walked quietly to where the action was taking place. He already knew it was supposed to happen in the barn, with broken hay bales scattered around to make a place for them to break their fall as the kiss got deeper.

"Don't think it's a good idea, you being here," Dino said, coming up beside him, walking at the same pace.

"Tough." His frustration needed some kind of outlet.

"Especially not with an attitude."

Tony stopped before they got in hearing range of the crew. "I have an attitude?"

Dino smiled. "Mr. Iverson won't think twice about kicking you off the set. You want that? You want Maggie to go through that humiliation?"

"No." They hadn't had a fight yet. He didn't want to start.

"Then go home."

"I can handle it."

"No, you can't. Trust me. I've watched it happen before. Not with Maggie," he added. "With lots of other couples. If you want to keep your sanity, you stay away during love scenes. It'll be bad enough watching it on-screen."

"I know what I can handle."

Dino shook his head several times, slowly. "I don't want to argue with you."

"Then don't." Tony started walking again. "You can come with me. If you see I can't handle it, you can take me out."

"Mr. Iverson's not gonna let you on set, Tony. I'm telling you to keep you from being embarrassed. Go home."

He knew the second Maggie realized he was there. She went completely still, even as someone was fluffing her hair and someone else was dusting her face with a makeup brush. She wore supertight jeans and a low-cut blouse. Other people turned to see what she was looking at.

Mac Iverson finally noticed. His shoulders slumped. Tucking his clipboard under his arm, he started toward Tony, but Maggie rushed up and stopped him, then walked the forty feet to Tony. Dino slipped away.

She gave Tony a hug, looking like a loving fiancée—if one didn't see her face.

"I'm leaving," he said before she started talking.

"This is business, Tony."

It bothered him that she didn't smile once. It showed she was pretty ticked off at him. "Any chance of you getting home early enough to go for a ride?" he asked.

"After this scene, I'll be done for the day."

"So, I should wait around?"

"There's a lot of setup and follow-up. It may only be thirty seconds in the movie, but it'll take a long time to film."

"Places, please," the director shouted.

Tony had to let her go do her job—kiss a man most women drooled over. "See you later," he said.

"Count on it."

He turned and walked away, not looking back. She'd moved into the barn by the time he got into his truck, started it and finally looked out the windshield.

Tony chewed himself out all the way back to the ranch. He was acting like a dumb teenager in...lust. His hormones had been overriding his common sense ever since she'd moved in.

Hell, he'd never experienced a flicker of jealousy before, and here he was, making a fool of himself and putting pressure on her, embarrassing her in front of the people she worked with. She'd already had enough gossip to deal with.

Time to rein back, he decided. He wished he'd come to

that conclusion before he'd driven himself to the set without thinking it through.

Better late than never.

Once again Tony was behaving differently, Maggie thought, but this time it was a swing to the other direction—less attentive and less solicitous. She would like to know why, but didn't really want to spoil their ride if the answer was something she didn't want to hear.

They'd ridden for quite a while across open range, side by side, but now she followed him up a narrow trail, her well-trained mare picking her way. Maggie could identify more of the flora now, not just the mesquite, but the prickly pear cactus, a spiny shrub called a crucifixion thorn, piñon juniper and other desert scrub.

She appreciated the harsh beauty of the surroundings but also Tony, the way he sat in the saddle, how he carried himself. The way he surveyed his land, pride in his posture and what little she could see of his expression now and then. He was king of this piece of the world, and he wore the crown well, even if it was black and wool and shaped like a Stetson—although in deference to the heat today, he was wearing a straw hat, had instructed her to, as well.

Her survival skills were nonexistent here, but he could handle any emergency, of that she was sure. She couldn't. She'd been sheltered, necessary in her position, and so well taken care of by other people that she didn't really know how to manage the details of life—hers were handled for her. Someone was always with her. She didn't have to be competent about anything but her work. Not that she never made a decision, but that she didn't have to. She'd rarely been in a supermarket because it usually resulted in a commotion.

Tony's competency was a turn-on for her. She liked that he identified himself as the Alpha dog of her pack, and that he followed through in his self-designated role. She sighed, content.

He turned around in the saddle. "You okay? You gettin' sore?"

"I'm fine. I'm happy."

"Don't want you walking bowlegged on set tomorrow." He watched her for a second longer then faced forward again.

She understood why he hadn't asked how her day went. He didn't want to know. She got that. But he seemed to be keeping her at arm's length completely, hadn't even kissed her hello, even though Butch and Sadie were right there, and he always kept up the loving fiancé routine in front of them. It had been awkward for Maggie when he hadn't at least hugged her. She'd tried to cover her discomfort by retreating to the bedroom right away, saying she needed to change clothes. But really, she just needed to be alone for a minute.

By the time she'd changed, he'd brought two saddled horses to the front of the house, and they mounted up and rode off with hardly a word spoken.

She'd never figured him for a moody man. A thoughtful one, yes, who went quiet frequently, but moody? Nope. But then, maybe the kiss last night had changed things for him.

It had for her. It had made her needy and on edge—and yet it also thrilled her, being desired like that. How could they keep going on, without doing something to relieve the frustration? Was it even realistic to expect it could, especially once the marriage vows were said?

"This is incredibly gorgeous scenery, Tony," she said, banishing the questions, wanting him to open up. "Can we stay until sunset?"

"Sure."

A few more minutes passed without conversation. They rode past an area overgrown with the crucifixion thornbushes, which reminded her of him at the moment—interesting to look at, but get too close and you get pricked.

They came to the top of a rise. She pulled up beside him. "Your land?"

"One of my pastures, but forest service land. We use it in January. It's the closest to the ranch and the lowest elevation."

"Where are your cattle?"

"Way up. Seven thousand feet. This is about four thousand. They're in the last pasture before we start cutting, sorting, weaning, preg checking, that kind of thing. Then it's off to market for the calves." He climbed down. So did she. He took both sets of reins and looped them over a branch.

They stood side by side and enjoyed the vista.

"I was way out of line today," he said finally. "Showing up on your set like that. I apologize."

Was that what had been bothering him? That he needed to apologize? He'd waited all this time to do so? "Thanks."

He kicked a rock loose. It bounced a couple of times. "I watched an old movie of yours this morning after you left."

Now they were getting to the heart of whatever was really bothering him. "Which one?"

"The Marriage Broker."

Probably the sexiest movie she'd done. It had a bedroom scene, although she'd stayed under the covers. But the kissing scene was long, with lots of close-ups. "What'd you think?"

"That I was glad I wasn't watching you film it."

Apparently he was admitting to some jealousy, after all.

"The one today wasn't nearly as…graphic as that one," she said.

"You hooked up with the other actor. John Henderson."

"For a while, yes. After the movie was over."

"It's not the first time that's happened with you."

"No." She put her hand on his arm. "But Rafe Valente is no threat, Tony. He's just my costar."

"How do you do that? How do you kiss someone and make it seem real when you don't feel it?"

"You just do. It's part of the job. But I think you're asking a deeper question than that. You're asking if I can fake it for the job, then could I fake it other times, too, right?"

She waited. He didn't answer, but he did look directly at her.

"I'm not faking it with you, Tony. It's honest with you."

"How do I know that? It looked real to me on the screen. I bought it."

"You're supposed to buy it or I haven't done my job. But remember, too, how you and I first got together. It was a choice. It was major attraction and trust and need. There was nothing fake about that."

"You were needy, I'll grant you that. But I think you were hurtin' a lot from Scott's breakup. It's not the same thing as really needing someone, now, is it?"

"I suppose not, but if you think I would've slept with you just because I was in pain—"

"And needed to forget for a while."

"That, too. But if you'll recall, I asked Leesa to find out who you were even before we met at the bar. I was attracted, period. I wouldn't have done anything about it if Scott hadn't ended things, but you got me going even before we talked."

"So, it was just animal attraction."

Was it? Could she explain it to him in a way that made sense? For her it had never been about animal attraction, but the whole deal—physical, emotional and intellectual. She knew it could be different for men.

"That night," she said, "I felt a pull toward you because of the man you are, inside. You helped me. Protected me. Got me away from the photographer without hesitation, even at your own inconvenience. But I wanted you bad." She touched his hand. "Maybe the bigger question is why did you sleep with me? You could've said no."

"I wanted you."

"It's that simple?"

"Something wrong with that, Margaret? I've had one-night stands before, although not in several years. When I woke up that morning and you were gone, at first I thought, hey, I like her style. You know, that *you* weren't much of one for mornings-after conversations, either."

"At first?"

"A fleeting thought, barely acknowledged." He brushed her hair back a little. "Because annoyance took over that you left without telling me."

She leaned into his hand. "You're my first one-night stand."

"I'm flattered?"

She smiled. "I'm thirty-one years old. You *should* be flattered."

"I ended up not being a one-night stand, so does it even count?"

"I guess you're right. My record is clean." She looked around. "Can we just sit here for a while?"

He walked to his horse, unstrapped a pack from the back of the saddle and brought it over. Inside was a blanket he spread on the ground, a couple of chicken sandwiches, apples and oatmeal-raisin cookies. He offered her a sandwich, and they sat in silence, eating.

"Tell me about your first kiss," she said. "First real kiss. One that counted."

His brows went up, but he answered. "Ginger Magnuson. We were fourteen. Happened in my parents' barn during a huge barbecue, with about a hundred guests."

"Did you enjoy it?"

"Course I did—once I got over being scared."

She looked off into the horizon. "Mine involved a lot of people, too, and my first kiss was also when I was fourteen. It was on the set of the television series I was doing at the time, my second series. I'd started when I was five with one show, which lasted six years. Then at thirteen I started another, for a five-year run." She met his interested gaze. "My first kiss was in front of all the cast and crew, and then some, with a boy I despised. Fortunately the writers ended that storyline and for another year I was safe. Then they brought in another love interest, and I had to do it again. By the time I was eighteen and the series ended, I'd kissed five different boys, but none of them was a choice I made. It was just what the script called for. I didn't even have a real first date until I was twenty. Even then, I wasn't sure whether he'd asked out Maggie McShane the woman or Maggie McShane the star."

"I can see where that would be hard, especially as a teenager."

"And you're thinking I have no right to whine, because I chose my occupation, and that sort of thing comes with the territory of my business."

"I wasn't thinking that at all. I was thinking that childhood isn't all it's cracked up to be."

"Yours, too?"

He nodded.

"My experience made me a little jaded," she said.

"Would've done the same to me."

"Tony, you're the first man I ever thought was with me only because of who I am inside."

"Even Scott?"

She blew out a long breath, as if she'd just realized what she'd admitted. "After the fact, yes, even Scott."

He frowned, then he took her hand in his. "It was your outside that caught my attention, darlin'. Don't go thinkin' otherwise. But I came to like the person inside real fast, and like her more every day. I wasn't starstruck, if that's what you're saying, but I'm a man, Margaret. I appreciate how you look."

"Hey, *you're* my John Wayne."

"So, I'm fulfillin' some kind of fantasy for you?"

"Definitely. I had the hots for him before I even knew what the hots were."

He laughed, evidenced only by a small shaking of his shoulders and twinkle in his eyes.

"There's a quote attributed to John Wayne," she said. "Maybe you've heard it? 'Talk low, talk slow and don't say too much.' It's you."

"More my father, I think."

She tread carefully about the subject. "You and he seem to have…issues."

"You could say that."

She didn't know if she should question him further or let him tell her in his own time, but before she had a chance to ask, he said, "I'm not interested in talking about it, okay? It's a personal thing."

"Okay." Now what? Time to change the subject, she figured. Where could she take the conversation? "A week from Sunday I need to make a quick trip to San Francisco and check out the wedding arrangements. Do you want to come?"

"I'll be on the trail moving the herd from Friday to Monday."

"Oh. Okay."

"I thought everything was being handled for you."

"It is. But Garnet's been telling me that the company building the hotel, Taka-Hanson, is being sued. It's pretty messy, apparently."

"Like what? Enough that the wedding might not happen?"

"It's been big stuff. Accusations of graft, talk of lawsuits against senior management. I'd just like to see for myself that everything is in place. Besides which, my friend Jenny Warren, the one who asked me to have the wedding at The Taka San Francisco in the first place, will be flying in from Chicago with her husband for the weekend. She's pregnant, and it's probably the last time she can safely fly before she gives birth, so she won't be coming to the wedding. Two trips too close together. I'd like to see her."

"Whatever you need to do is fine with me. You know that."

She did. So, why had she felt a need to justify the trip? And why was she disappointed he wouldn't be going along? She wanted Jenny to meet him.

After a moment the reality she'd temporarily forgotten imploded, almost blinding her. She was thinking about him as long-term. As a real partner, husband, lover—forever. But that wasn't the case. It was a here-and-now marriage, one with purpose. One of convenience…

A marriage of convenience. Now *there* was an anachronism.

Maggie gathered up the empty food wrappings and stuck them in the large plastic bag they'd been in. "Thanks for thinking to bring dinner with you."

He nodded. "Do you cook?"

"I wouldn't starve, but it's not a passion. My specialty is scrambled eggs." Big deal, she thought. Anyone could do that. But she'd also never cleaned her own house. Had never paid a bill or balanced a checkbook. She didn't even make her own bed.

"What's running through your head?" Tony asked.

"How few domestic skills I have."

"Is it something you aspire to?" His tone was wry.

"I don't know. I feel very…unwifely."

"I figure it's safe to say it wouldn't be expected of you, given your schedule and place in the world. But if you'd like to give it a shot, I wouldn't mind seeing you in a cute little white apron."

"And nothing else?"

"Maybe some four-inch heels."

"Fishnet stockings?"

"Sounds good. And a garter belt." He eyed her legs. "You've got the legs for it." He lifted his gaze. "Ever had sex in the great outdoors?"

"No." Why was he asking? Did he intend to—

"Outdoors adds a little extra kick. It's the danger element. Wild animals. People."

She got it now. He was teasing her, trying to lighten the mood. They were out for a picnic, a break from routine. Their conversation shouldn't be so serious.

"Speaking of danger," she said, then touched a scar on his forehead that arrowed into his hair. "You really got banged up rodeoing, didn't you?"

"That? Hell. That's nothin'. I've broken a lot of bones. Some have healed well. Some haven't. I know it's gonna rain long before it does."

A thrashing noise reached her, starting a distance away but coming closer in a hurry. It blurred past.

"It's just a buck." There was a smile in his voice.

"I know. I've seen pictures." She continued to scout the terrain.

"Pictures, huh? Okay."

"Don't tease me."

"Why not? It's fun."

"I feel like such a city slicker."

"You are. But what's wrong with that?"

She shrugged, but was still watchful.

"There are herds of elk and deer and antelope all over," he said. "Lots of eagles and coyotes, too."

She looked harder at the underbrush. "Coyotes?"

"Yep. The Lucky Hand adjoins a wilderness area." He rolled up the blanket and fastened it to his saddle then brought her horse to her and cupped his hands for her to step up. He mounted his own horse, then moved it close to her, leaned across and kissed her lightly. "This was good."

An understatement. They'd resolved a few issues, shared a few confidences. "Yes. Thank you, cowboy."

"You're mighty welcome, ma'am," he drawled in a pretty good imitation of the Duke. He tipped his hat then urged his horse toward the trail, leaving her to follow, a stupid grin on her face, happier than she'd been in, well, forever.

"When we get back to the ranch, I'll be heading to Phoenix for the evening. My monthly poker game," he said. "You shouldn't wait up."

"I can't come?"

"Well, that'd sorta be like me showing up on your set today."

"Oh. It's a *serious* game."

"You could say that."

"What do you play?"

"Texas hold'em."

"Do you win?"

"More often than not."

"Oh, yeah. You won the ranch in a poker game."

He was quiet a little while, then he reined his horse a little closer to hers. "Here's something only Butch knows. The man I won the ranch from, he had cancer. Knew he was dying. He had no family. He'd sponsored me at the beginning of my rodeo career, and I knew I was ready to give up the circuit and settle down. He had a winning hand—I knew it, he knew it, but he folded, leaving the deed on the table. A month later he was gone. I think he liked the romance of giving up his ranch that way. People would talk about it. About him. And me, I suppose."

It seemed like such an old-fashioned thing to have happened, but Maggie was getting used to the fact that some things didn't change here as fast as elsewhere. In a good way.

"So, you were like a son to him?" she asked.

"Not exactly, but we admired each other. And he and my dad had knocked heads a few times. He wanted the ranch to survive and thought I'd make a good caretaker."

"He was right."

"Yeah, he was right. Anyway, sometimes the poker games last all night. I don't want you worrying if I'm not home when you wake up."

She smiled slowly. "And if you do get home early

enough, will I know if you won or lost by whether or not you wake me up and make mad, passionate love to me?"

What are you doing, teasing him like that? Her mind echoed with the repercussions of such teasing, especially when he got all serious-looking.

"I'd venture to say under normal circumstances I'd do that either way it turned out. These aren't normal circumstances."

He looked questioningly at her, as if she could change those circumstances, if she wanted.

She wanted. She just couldn't. "So, how will I know if you won or lost?" she asked.

After a moment, he looked ahead. "You won't."

"You'll keep it a secret."

"That's right."

"Why?"

"Because some things are sacred, Margaret."

"Poker winnings are *sacred?*" She laughed.

"Obviously you have no love of the game if you doubt that."

"Oh, I've played a bit in my time."

"Are you as good as you are at pool?"

She smiled.

"I sense a challenge in that smile," he said.

"I'm pretty competitive."

"I've noticed. Want to have a little race?" He pointed ahead. "To the rock that looks like a buffalo?"

She slanted him a look. "I figure you know you can win, hands down. You know these horses."

"That would be cheating. I don't cheat."

She laughed. "Well, I'll have to say no, thanks, anyway, because my contract forbids it. I can't do more than trot, unless it's while we're filming."

"They sure do think of everything."

"Insurance is expensive."

"When your film is done, then."

"It's a date. But I'm choosing my own horse."

"You don't trust me?"

"I've proven that already, cowboy. I trusted you with my secrets and my reputation."

He turned in his saddle and gave her a long, heated look. "And your body."

She caught her breath at his look—and discovered she didn't have a response.

He did, however—a slow, sure, satisfied smile that seemed to say, "It's just a matter of time."

Chapter Ten

Tony had decided against replacing himself with hired help to move the cattle. No matter how efficient the hand was, Tony was still the boss, and he needed to see for himself how his herd was faring, especially the last month before he'd be sending the heifers to market. He knew every one of his cows personally, individually. People outside the business could never understand that, but it was true.

Another truth was he needed a break from Maggie. A week had passed since their ride. Tension was building nightly as they denied themselves physical release. It had become hard to imagine his life before he had met her. Was that only three weeks ago?

"I won't smell too sweet when I return," he said to her as she gathered her script pages from the bedside table. She was dressed and ready to head to the set. He was about to leave, too.

"I'll be sure to get myself downwind of you," she said.

"You learn fast."

"Better believe it." She came up to him, almost laid a hand on his chest, then dropped it. "It's going to seem really strange around here without you."

"Well, there is that little visit with my mother to keep you occupied." He got a kick out of the way she tried to seem okay about entertaining his mother and sister for dinner tonight, but he knew she was nervous.

"Lucky for her that Sadie's cooking," Maggie said, trying to form a smile. "Can I give them all the info on flying to San Francisco next week for the wedding?"

"Sure. You behave yourself."

"While the bull's away…" She grinned.

"Uh-huh." He took her hand, then they left the bedroom and headed to the front porch. Sadie joined them.

Butch came up the steps. "All set, boss." He took Sadie into his arms and kissed her, a long, passionate kiss, then rubbed her belly. "Take care of our baby girl."

"Hell, Butch, you're leavin' for four measly hours," Tony said.

"Four hours?" Maggie repeated. "What do you mean?"

"Butch is hauling the trailer with our horses to where we'll start off. It'd take all day to ride there. He's coming right back home. Someone's gotta oversee things here."

"So, what'll you be doing up there?"

"Riding circles around the pasture, mostly to close the gates that the recreationalists leave open. Seeing what fences need repairing. And move the cattle, of course." He could see she was questioning why he had to go. "It's *my* herd."

"I know. I *understand*. How's the cell phone reception?"

"There's a couple of trees we can stand under that sometimes get reception." He saw worry—or something—settle in her eyes. He didn't want to read too much into it.

"How do we get in touch with you, if something comes up?" she asked.

"Butch'll know how."

He kissed her. Not as long or dramatically as Butch had kissed Sadie, but good enough for public consumption, although not good enough for personal satisfaction. "See you in a few days, darlin'. Don't fret, okay? You have a good trip to San Francisco. Let's go, Butch. You're holdin' us up."

They'd almost reached the truck when Dino walked over.

"Everything good?" Tony asked.

"Nothing unexpected."

"Okay. Don't hesitate to have Butch track me down, if necessary."

"Yes, sir."

"Sorry. I know I don't need to tell you how to do your job."

"No, sir."

Tony was grateful that Dino was there to watch over Maggie. She seemed oblivious to the strange vehicles that had made their way onto the property since she'd moved in. "And you're going to San Francisco with her."

"Yes. I'm leaving the rest of the crew in place, though. She hasn't announced she's going, so my hope is that she can fly in, do her business and fly out that night without calling attention to herself. If the crew here sticks to their routine, it'll be a good diversion."

"Do all movie stars need this kind of protection?"

"Depends. Some don't keep security with them all the time. But Maggie's a pretty easy target. Maybe I should show you some of the mail she gets, so you know what we're always on the alert for."

Would it always be like that? Tony wondered. Her whole life? What a way to live. "Yeah, gather some of that. I'd like to see it. You don't show them to her?"

"Only if something looks like a real threat. It's happened. She handles it well. Does what I tell her to. She's been in the spotlight her whole life. She knows it comes with the territory."

"Most people would rebel at some point."

Dino smiled. "I would have thought you'd figured out by now that she's not most people."

"Touché." He squeezed Dino's shoulder. "Do you ever take a vacation?"

"Life with Maggie McShane is one constant vacation."

He appreciated Dino's dry wit. "Talk to you later." He looked back at the house, but Maggie wasn't on the porch. She couldn't have left yet, since Dino would be driving her.

Tony ignored the twinge that she wasn't there waving goodbye to him. Even if theirs was a true relationship, he wouldn't expect her to be "the little woman."

It was an entirely old-fashioned notion, and he was an entirely modern man.

Except all week he'd been fantasizing about her wearing a little white apron…

"Did my new clothes arrive?" Maggie asked Leesa when they got back to the ranch that evening.

"They're in the back of the car. I asked the shopkeeper to press them and put them on hangers."

"Good, thanks. How much time do I have before Sue-Ellen and Mary Beth arrive?"

"Half an hour."

"Is that all? I need to hurry. Don't want to keep them

waiting. I'll take a quick shower, if you'll bring my new outfit."

"You've met presidents and royalty with less anxiety," Leesa commented.

"I know. It's stupid. They were both so nice to me at the barbecue. But Tony was sitting next to me the whole time, too." She rushed up the porch steps and into the house. She waved to Sadie, who was lighting candles in the living room. "Everything okay?"

"Right on schedule."

Maggie walked backward toward the master suite. "Did Tony get up to the pasture okay?"

"Right on schedule."

"Good. Are you sure you won't join us for dinner?" Maggie asked hopefully. The more, the merrier, she'd thought. Anything to deflect attention. Even Leesa had excused herself.

Sadie laughed. "Sue-Ellen won't make you feel uncomfortable," she said. "She's a true lady."

"If you say so."

"Now, Mary Beth, on the other hand…"

"Great. Thanks." She heard Sadie laugh again.

Maggie rushed through her shower, applied light makeup, then slipped into her new long denim skirt and embroidered blouse. She'd bought dressier boots, and fastened a gorgeous silver-and-turquoise belt at her waist.

One might think you were entertaining a real mother-in-law, a little voice in her head said.

Women's laughter drifted from the living room. Her guests had arrived. She closed her eyes and took a few deep breaths, settling herself, trying to banish her guilt at marrying Tony when she knew it was temporary. She wished she could confide in his mother and sister so that they wouldn't hate her when the truth came out, but she knew Tony would have a fit if she did that.

Why is it so important that everyone likes you?

The question ran through her head as she headed to greet the women. She'd been vaguely aware of her need for universal acceptance for a while, but particularly the past few weeks. It was more than honoring her parents and grandparents. It was a deep-down need. But why?

She stopped in her tracks. Maybe a more important question was why she hadn't let Scott be the bad guy to the public? Was she looking to change her image? If so, why?

Because even though she hadn't wanted to let Jenny down by canceling the wedding at The Taka San Francisco, they could have figured out something to make up for it. Some other significantly star-studded event to launch the hotel.

It came down to the reason why she'd agreed to marry Scott in the first place—she hungered for family and stability. But there had to be more to it than that. Maybe she should go into therapy and find out. Most of her friends in the business had at one point or another.

Maggie straightened her shoulders and stepped into the living room. "I'm so glad you're here."

"Thanks for being gracious enough to say yes when we invited ourselves," Mary Beth said. "We figured we trapped you but good."

"*You* invited. *You* figured," Sue-Ellen said. "I only heard about it after she'd invited us. I hope you don't feel pressured, Maggie."

"Oh, no. Not at all."

Sadie snickered.

"Much," Maggie amended with a smile. "Would you

like a glass of wine before dinner? I see Sadie's made some wonderful appetizers."

They settled on sofas in front of the coffee table with the food, a small spread of light hors d'oeuvres, the kind of things men would gripe about as being rabbit food.

Sue-Ellen passed Maggie a photo album she'd set on the table. "I thought you'd like to see pictures of Tony growing up."

"Oh, I'd love to! Thank you for thinking of it."

"I wanted to show you when you came for the barbecue, but Tony would've taken it away and hidden it forever. He was a cute little rascal, wasn't he?"

"Adorable." Maggie turned pages slowly. Two things jumped out at her. He wasn't smiling in the pictures, so it wasn't a recent thing with him. And in every family shot he stood off on his own a little, while the rest of the family gathered close.

"Stubborn cuss," Sue-Ellen said. "Always did things his own way. Didn't even talk until he had something to say."

"What do you mean?"

"We couldn't coax him to say words like Mama or Dada or any of the usual first words. Doctor checked his hearing, then said to leave him be, that he'd come around in his own time. He was right. When Tony was almost three, he said, 'I'm hungry. When's dinner?' And that was the beginning."

"Opened the floodgates," Mary Beth said.

"Really? He talked a lot?"

"Hard to believe, huh? Then when he was about twelve, he stopped."

"I don't think Maggie needs all our family history just yet," Sue-Ellen said, setting a hand on her daughter's arm.

"Well, I'm interested, unless there's some reason you

can't say," Maggie said, seeing them exchange glances. "I don't want to talk behind Tony's back. Obviously I noticed he doesn't talk a whole lot, but he says what's necessary. And I like how he thinks."

"The change in him happened overnight," Sue-Ellen said. "We chalked it up to adolescence, but I'm thinking it was something else. I asked him. He wouldn't say."

Maggie turned a page and saw him at about age six or seven, sitting on a horse, looking serious and all cowboy, even then. "He completely stopped talking?"

"No. He started saying only what was necessary, as you called it. He's like Hoyt that way," Sue-Ellen said. "Not that Tony would like to hear that."

Maggie wondered if she could ask questions about Tony's relationship with his father then decided it would be disloyal. "I'm used to men who talk about themselves a lot," she said, guiding the conversation down a slightly different path. "Tony doesn't brag. I wouldn't have known how many rodeo titles he'd won if I hadn't seen his trophy case. And I use that term lightly, since it amounts to a simple glass cabinet hidden away in his office, not out where anyone could see it. I had no idea he started when he was seven."

"Riding sheep," Sue-Ellen said.

"I would've loved to have seen that."

"Where do you keep your awards?" Mary Beth asked.

"I don't have any, except for charitable work. Never been nominated, even. I've always done kind of lightweight stuff."

"Do you want to do something else?"

"I think almost everyone in the arts wants to push themselves to do more, do better. To stretch. It's easy to get into a rut and stay where it's comfortable." And she'd been in a rut for a while now. She'd enjoyed filming this particular movie because of Mac, a director she admired, but she found herself increasingly antsy with the whole hurry-up-and-wait process. Between scenes she'd go to her trailer, where Leesa would get after her for pacing and fidgeting, something she never did.

But she knew what prompted the change. She wanted to be at home. With Tony. She didn't want to be on the set. She didn't want to be kissing Rafe Valente, who used too much tongue and not enough finesse. She wanted Tony's mouth, his taste, his heat, his intensity.

Maggie felt her face warming and quickly returned her focus to the photo album, which included newspaper clippings of his rodeo events, from age seven on. She encountered a blank page and looked at Sue-Ellen in question. "Let me guess. His ex-wife?"

"I didn't take the picture out because of you," she said. "I took it out years ago. Should've put something else in there, but I forgot."

Maggie was curious about what his ex looked like.

"We didn't like her," Mary Beth said.

"Tony told me."

"Mom and I are really interested in how you and Tony met."

"Are you?" Maggie smiled. "I don't mean to be coy, but we decided not to share that. I can only tell you that he came to my rescue, was an absolute gentleman when another man might have taken advantage and then everything happened so fast it's all a blur. I think he's an amazing man. One of a kind."

"Love at first sight?"

"Mary Beth," Sue-Ellen said, "leave her alone. She said it's private. Let's respect that."

Maggie made the decision right then to tell Tony's family the truth when they ended the marriage. He wouldn't be made to be the heavy—not to them.

"I promise I'll share more later, but it's all kind of new and tender right now," Maggie said.

"Dinner's served," Sadie said.

Maggie spent a good part of the evening answering questions from Mary Beth about show business—the actors, behind-the-scenes information, separating fact from fiction. Maggie, in turn, peppered the women with questions about living on a ranch, dealing with the isolation and hard work, separating fact from fiction for her, as well.

"I think much of the mythology of the American cowboy is as true now as ever," Sue-Ellen said. "They're hardworking, honest men. They don't make a lot of money. They do it because they love it and can't see themselves doing anything else. Some of them try, usually for a woman, but most of 'em have a hard time adjusting to life off the range."

"It's been eye-opening for me," Maggie said. They were lingering over chocolate-espresso cake and coffee. "I always pictured cattle barons. Big, huge spreads owned and run by generations of families, who made a lot of money doing it. Like in that movie *Giant*."

"We're a rare breed in that our ranch is our own, and two of our sons work it with us. But none of us ranchers can make it on cattle alone. Everyone has to subsidize in some way. We've all done other kinds of work, when necessary. Both my daughters-in-law have part-time jobs in Sedona. Hoyt and the boys have always trained and stabled horses."

"Tony seems to have other things going, as well."

"He's been even more innovative. He writes grants to

get money to help keep the land environmentally sound in ways that also help his business. He and Butch are starting a trail-ride business. He's been talking about starting a winery, of all things, even raising grass-fed beef as a niche market product. That boy is plumb full of ideas."

Tony Young, entrepreneur. It made Maggie smile. She never saw him hard at work, just always knew he'd been working hard while she was off working. She loved learning about this side of him, the side he wouldn't have talked about much, she suspected.

"Look at the time," Sue-Ellen said suddenly. "We'd best be getting home."

"Do you have to drive back to Scottsdale tonight?" Maggie asked Mary Beth.

"No, I'll stay at the ranch. My kids are old enough to get themselves off to school okay without me. For a day, anyway. This was really fun, Maggie, thank you."

"For me, too. We'll do it again."

There were hugs goodbye, then she stood on the porch, waving as they pulled away.

She'd told Sadie to go to bed an hour ago, so she cleared the dining-room table, loaded the dishwasher, probably incorrectly, then was headed to the bedroom when someone knocked on the door.

Butch stood there, as well as Dino. Butch was holding up some kind of transmitter. "Tony wants to talk to you. Just push this button when you want to talk, then let go of it so you can hear him. You can keep it with you. I'll get it from you in the morning."

"I thought he said— Never mind. Thanks."

She waited until she got into the bedroom before she pressed the button, even though he kept saying her name every few seconds, and added instructions on what to do in order to talk.

"So, I guess you're under a good-reception tree, hmm?" she said, dripping sarcasm.

"The transmitters are a recent purchase. Smoke signals and birdcalls weren't too reliable."

She refused to laugh, so she didn't key the mike.

"I just wanted to be able to surprise you tonight," he said.

That took the wind out of her sails. He really was sweet. "Well, you did."

"How'd it go? And before you answer, you should know this isn't private."

"Really, Tony, you could've said that right at the start. I could've embarrassed myself."

"I would've interrupted."

Was he laughing? She was pretty sure he was laughing.

"Did Mary Beth wear you out with questions?" he asked.

She didn't want anyone who might be listening to think she was being stuck-up. "She asked a lot. I answered a few. You sure were a cute little tyke in your red cowboy hat." He still looked cute, especially wearing those leather chaps that emphasized what a great butt he had.

"Which means that Mom brought the photo album."

He'd probably groaned, but hadn't keyed up yet so she could hear him. "She did," Maggie said. "I loved it."

"What other secrets did she reveal?"

"Just favorite mother/son stories. Nothing embarrassing. That'll come at another time, I think, when we've settled in with each other. She didn't let the cat out of the bag about anything."

"She's a smart woman. She knows that puttin' that cat back in is just about impossible."

She laughed, remembering to key up so that he heard.

"So you had a good time?" he asked.

"I had a great time, Tony. They're wonderful women. Very genuine. How's everything where you are?"

"Had to round up more strays than usual. Had some broken fence."

She loved knowing he was there, within voice range, but she wanted to tell him she missed him—because she did. She was sitting on the great big bed she'd shared with him for three weeks.

"You there, Margaret?"

She wanted to feel his arms around her, to sleep snuggled up to him, as she had been. "I'm here."

"You must be tired."

"I still have to learn lines."

"Oh. Sorry. I didn't realize. I'll let you go. Sweet dreams."

She didn't want to let him go. "Tony?"

"What, darlin'?"

"Stay safe."

"I will. Don't you worry. I've done this more times'n I can count."

"Okay. Good night."

"Night. I'll give you a buzz tomorrow night, unless you've got plans."

"I was thinkin' about goin' into town and playin' a round or two of pool at the Red Rock Saloon," she teased.

"For old times' sake?" he asked, his tone unreadable.

"Trip down memory lane."

"Short trip, considering."

She could tell he was smiling. "I'll be here. Call when you can, cowboy."

"You need me during the night, just push the button and start talkin', okay? I'll hear you."

Just knowing that made her relax. Really, when had she become so dependent? "Okay. Later, then."

"G'night."

She hugged the transmitter before setting it on the bedside table. After a minute she got up, changed into her nightgown, grabbed her script pages and crawled into bed.

When she woke up in the morning, she was wrapped around his pillow.

Chapter Eleven

Maggie sat back and enjoyed the view as she, Dino and Leesa were driven from the airport to downtown San Francisco Sunday morning. Maggie adored the City by the Bay. She loved the marine fog that turned everything gray until midday. She wallowed in the salty ocean breezes that scented the air, was fascinated by the unique architecture, the gawking tourists and the noisy crowds at Fisherman's Wharf.

As cities went, it was entirely individual. She'd been thinking for a while about selling her Malibu house and buying a place in the San Francisco area, renting space in L. A. only when she needed to be there for long periods of time. Leesa's wish to keep their home base in L.A.—where the action was, according to her—had delayed Maggie from going ahead with her plan. Dino hadn't weighed in, saying only that he served at the pleasure of Maggie McShane, as if she were president or something, which had made her laugh.

Since she hadn't taken either Leesa or Dino into her confidence about the truth of her impending marriage, Maggie figured they probably thought she would be living at the Lucky Hand, at least during her breaks. She wondered how they felt about that. Dino would never ask if that was her plan. Leesa would, in time.

Maggie didn't have answers herself yet, so she hoped Leesa put off asking for a while.

When Maggie stopped to think about it, it was strange how few plans she had for her life at this point, a life that was usually booked for two years in advance. She had the indie movie next month, then a feature film in six months. Filming for the current movie had ended yesterday, so unless they needed any reshoots, she had several days to rest and play before they headed back to San Francisco next weekend for the wedding. She wanted to ride a lot more, to see all of Tony's land, owned and leased. To have that race they'd talked about. And to see the cattle, which she hadn't yet.

"Where are you and Tony going on your honeymoon?" Leesa asked, breaking into Maggie's pleasant thoughts.

Honeymoon? How amazing—neither she nor Tony had brought it up. "Um. Not decided yet."

Dino sat up a little.

"What?" she asked him, knowing he'd reacted in some way. "Did Tony tell you something?"

He squirmed. "No, I— I'm sure you'd be the one to know."

"He did, didn't he?" She leaned toward him. "Where's he taking me?"

"I couldn't say." His expression closed up.

She knew that look. She wouldn't get any information out of him.

Was Tony really planning a honeymoon? He shouldn't be spending money on something so frivolous. She'd be happy at the ranch…

But he would seem like less than a loving bridegroom. She shouldn't be surprised. He'd been protective of her reputation from the first night, her chivalrous cowboy.

"There's the hotel," Leesa said, pointing ahead. "Wow. Talk about soaring. It's touching the clouds."

The building was all silvery-gray concrete and glass, a modern structure that shone like a jewel amid other glittering buildings around it.

Leesa had called ahead, so when their limo pulled into the hotel entry, three people were already there to greet them, including Jenny Warren, Maggie's friend.

Maggie's heart skipped a beat or two at seeing Jenny in her seventh month of pregnancy. She hadn't tamed her copper-colored hair in a knot as she used to, but left it down and flowing. She looked…maternal, one hand resting on her abdomen.

They hugged. Maggie felt the hard, round cradle of pregnancy press against her, creating a longing inside her that had been surfacing a lot lately.

Jenny hooked her arm through Maggie's, and they moved toward the building. Around them last-minute construction continued, a cacophony of equipment and workers, then the two women stepped into the hotel itself, all modern and stylish. Although quieter than outside, it echoed with construction sounds, as well.

"You look gorgeous, as always," Jenny said.

"So do you. You've got the pregnancy glow I've always heard about."

"I'm starting to waddle. I hate that." She grinned, her

eyes sparkling. "Richard has been so sweet. So complimentary. But I know I'm walking funny. Hi, Dino. Hey, Leesa," she said to the pair that followed. "Dino, the security chief will be with you in just a minute. He'll give you a tour. And, Leesa, here comes the wedding planner, Andrea, who will show you the suites and answer any of your questions."

With that business settled, Jenny took Maggie to Ally Rogers's office, the interior designer who'd been hired the month before to finish up the decorating after the original designer was found to be taking kickbacks and bribes. She'd inherited a huge job, since it meant taking over the Kyoto site, too.

"I have to say, Jenny, the negative publicity about the company being sued made me wonder if the wedding would happen here."

"I don't think a tsunami could've stopped this wedding. It's being handled, Maggie. As soon as our CFO Tom Holloway discovered that Taka-Hanson was being sued by that fired employee for wrongful termination, he hired a great attorney, Eric Nelson, to defend the company. He's an old law school friend of Jack Hanson. Believe me, there won't be a scandal surrounding your wedding."

Except maybe my own, Maggie thought. "You realize that none of those names ring any bells with me."

Jenny laughed. "Sorry. I get carried away with the family business sometimes. So—on to more interesting things. Ally told me you two know each other."

"She redid my house in Malibu last year. She's a dream to work with."

"And so much in love."

"Really? I hadn't heard that."

They entered the office. Ally, her honey-blond hair shimmering over her shoulders, came around her desk, her hands extended. She was a designer to the stars, but could've been a star herself, given her curvaceous body and gorgeous face.

Jenny said she'd be back to get Maggie later and they would have time to catch up, then have an early dinner with Richard before Maggie's flight home. She left Maggie alone with Ally then.

"Jenny tells me you have news," Maggie said. "Something about being in love?"

Her eyes went a little dreamy. "His name is Jake. We're engaged."

"That's wonderful. When's the wedding?"

"We haven't set a date. He lives in Chicago, so we're trying to figure things out. I'm sure I'll be moving there, but right now it's a whirlwind. I can't wait, though. Come on. Let me show you this magnificent building."

Beginning a thorough tour, Ally grabbed a notebook and led Maggie into the grand ballroom, an elegant, cosmopolitan room with high ceilings, sleek chandeliers and a large dance floor. Ally showed Maggie renderings of how the room would look decorated—not tons of roses but unusual orchids, a variety of species and colors. Maggie wondered how Tony would react to the nontraditional design—if he even cared about such things.

"An entire staff has been devoted strictly to your wedding and reception," Ally said. "You know the hotel isn't officially open yet, but we have enough guest rooms prepared for all your guests." She gave Maggie a detail-by-detail rundown of the event as they toured the hotel, including the kitchen.

"So, I know you and Jenny are friends," Ally said as they made their way back to her office. "May I ask how you met?"

"I was in Japan doing a film, maybe four years ago? Jenny was a society reporter at the *Tokyo Tribune* trying to be acknowledged as a 'serious' journalist, and she covered a party I attended. I'd escaped to a private garden for a little break from the crush, and she followed me, and quite efficiently and charmingly talked me into giving her an exclusive interview." Maggie smiled, remembering how determined Jenny had been. "We just liked each other, and stayed in touch ever since."

"Then she heard you were getting married and offered the hotel for the ceremony?"

"Offered my name to Helen Taka-Hanson, anyway, as an opportunity to open the hotel with a big PR splash. It was good timing, all around. Symbiotic."

"Definitely for the hotel," Ally said. "And now you're living on a ranch. Need a decorator to make it yours?"

Maggie pictured Tony's reaction to that. "I wouldn't dream of changing anything yet. I do expect to have more work for you at some point, but not until I figure out my housing situation, what to keep, what to sell. I'm not going to make any quick decisions."

Their long trek brought them back to Ally's office. "Let me give Jenny a buzz, and see if she's ready," Ally said. "That is, if you feel all your questions have been answered, and everything is to your satisfaction."

"It looks exquisite, Ally. Thank you so much. I knew Jenny would keep an eye on things, but it wasn't her job except as a friend. And with the pregnancy, it was too much to ask. As soon as I heard you were taking charge and would be here a lot, I knew I wouldn't have to worry."

"Well, as I said, I'm just the hub of a great big wheel of competency, including an official wedding planner. We've had the best people working on everything. It'll be a showcase for them, too, so they've gone all out."

"I'm glad I don't see the bill," Maggie said, smiling. "Garnet's lined up someone to buy rights to the first photos, I understand. We had a huge argument about it."

"Can't buck the system. It's the norm for a celebrity wedding these days. At least this way you'll get approval of the photos they run."

Maggie moved to the window as Ally made the call to Jenny, but there wasn't much to see from the low level. She wondered how Tony was going to feel about the photos being sold. She probably should've consulted him, because she was pretty sure he wouldn't know it was the "norm."

"I've had a light snack sent up to the suite, since we'll be having an early dinner," Jenny said a few minutes later as they took the elevator to the top floor.

"Where are Leesa and Dino?"

"Leesa's waiting in the suite. I think she wants to be turned loose to do some shopping. Dino's doing what Dino does. Got his nose in every corner of the building, checking for security flaws. I don't think he'll find any. We've guaranteed that the president could stay here."

"Which should be enough for Dino, but won't be," Maggie said, as the elevator door opened into a large, airy living room space, complete with piano. The view of the city was unrivaled, encompassing bridges and the Bay and peaks and valleys, plus the incredible skyline unmatched anywhere else in the world.

She sent Leesa on her way, asked her to be back by five o'clock, then settled in with Jenny to eat from a tray of fruit and cheese. They enjoyed a long, easy conversation. Maggie wished she could share the truth with Jenny—with anyone. With every passing day she'd felt more pressure, more stress from hiding and pretending.

Later, Jenny's husband joined them for dinner. Maggie had met Richard only once, but his love for his wife hadn't dimmed with time. "Tall, dark and handsome" described him, but the way his gaze went tender upon seeing Jenny was indescribable—and made Maggie feel alone. Oh, Tony was wonderful to her, but he never looked at her like she was the most precious thing in his life.

And why should he?

Why should he, indeed. They'd made a business arrangement. The fact they'd been so sexually compatible normally would be a bonus. They hadn't argued about anything, probably because of the short-term deal. Why waste time and energy on arguing?

But I want him to look at me like Richard looks at Jenny...

In the middle of San Francisco-style dinner of clam chowder, crab legs and sourdough bread—and roast chicken for Jenny—Richard got a phone call. He excused himself, not returning for about ten minutes, then sat down to finish dinner.

"That was Steven. My brother," he added to Maggie. "Caitlin, his twelve-year-old daughter, is giving him trouble."

"What kind of trouble?" Jenny asked.

"She got herself mixed up with the wrong crowd, and is rebelling, big time."

"It's tough to lose your mother when you're so young. What's he going to do?" Jenny asked.

"I'm supposed to talk to you about it." Richard's eyes twinkled.

"This must be the day people need my sterling advice. Remember my friend Samara? Maggie, I think you met her in Japan, too, didn't you?"

"The photographer?"

"Right. She's decided to move to the States and wondered if I could help her get settled."

"That's a big move," Richard said.

Maggie sat back and sipped her iced tea as they talked. Richard and Jenny lived a regular life. They worked, ate meals together, talked about normal things. What would it be like not to be in the spotlight? Maggie wondered. To have a sibling ask for help regarding a troubled child? To have a friend want her help with a move to a new country? To have a normal how-was-your-day conversation?

What would it be like to be married and have children and a life without paparazzi or the need for a bodyguard? Not to have her garbage rummaged through and her every move documented?

Family and security. It wasn't just her dream anymore but a craving, and yet she'd set herself up in a situation where she would only go through the motions of marriage then head to divorce court. And for what? To protect her image? Yes. Future roles? Definitely.

But also because of Tony, who had come to her rescue and to whom she'd promised a payoff. He'd kept her secret, his end of the bargain. She owed him her commitment to their deal. After all, she was honest and reliable and steady. America's Sweetheart. Little did people know...

She felt bad about misleading his family, too, who'd accepted her easily, getting over their awe quickly. It was what she'd missed—a big, noisy family. How could she give them up, too?

Jenny waved a hand in front of Maggie's face. "Daydreaming about Tony?" Jenny asked.

Maggie smiled. "Always."

At least that wasn't a lie.

It was almost eleven o'clock by the time Dino pulled the SUV up in front of the ranch house. The front porch light was on, welcoming them, even though inside it would be empty. She should've stayed in San Francisco overnight, Maggie thought, as she climbed the porch stairs, because then when she got home, Tony would be there. She didn't want to sleep alone another night.

Being with Jenny and Richard made her ache in ways she hadn't known she could.

Leesa said good-night and went to the guest room in the back corner of the house. Maggie went into the kitchen and poured a glass of water, then grabbed a chocolate chip cookie from a rearing-palomino cookie jar. She turned off the light and stood in the dark nibbling on the cookie, looking out the window. The lights were off in Butch and Sadie's house across the way, but she figured they'd heard the car, had probably been waiting to hear it. The ranch was its own little world, everyone operating as a team, working hard, liking each other. She didn't sense any issues between people, no egos trying to take over.

It was an honest life.

Maggie made her way through the darkened house and into the bedroom. She set her purse on a nightstand, felt for the lamp switch—

"You're not downwind of me."

She jumped at Tony's words, then she swore, making him laugh, low and appreciative.

"Brat," she said, her heart still slamming against her sternum. "You could've turned on a light."

"Could've, sure." The bedding rustled as he sat up. "But what fun would that've been?"

Just the sound of his voice turned her to mush. She wanted him so much, wanted to feel what she'd felt that first night—that absolute freedom in his arms. The pure pleasure. The utter satisfaction. She was so tired of resisting, of behaving. She was done with being the good girl.

She wanted to be irresistible.

She made her way through the darkness until her fingers made contact with his bare chest. Without another moment's pause she kissed him, finding his mouth unerringly, her own hard and demanding—startling him, she could tell. She'd missed him so much. *So much*. He hadn't been off her mind for one second.

He turned on the bedside lamp, studied her for a few long moments, then pulled her onto the mattress and rolled her under him. "I think I'll go away more often," he murmured as she lifted up, going back for more, kissing him like she would never get another chance.

She didn't want him to go away ever again.

I love you, cowboy. The words stayed trapped in her mind, dazzled by the discovery, exalted by the revelation. She was glad he only wore briefs so that she didn't have to waste much time undressing him. She needed to feel his skin against hers, his legs tangling with hers, the absolute liberation to give and take and enjoy.

"I need you," she said. "If you say no, be prepared for an all-out seduction."

"Apparently you think you're talkin' to some other Tony Young," he murmured. "Although an all-out seduction sounds mighty tempting."

Which meant yes. She managed to get him to roll onto his back so that she could make a hungry trail down his body, tasting him everywhere, absorbing his heat, savoring his utter maleness, but wanting him now for the amazing and sexy man she'd come to know, not the fascinating and sexy stranger she'd desired before. She slid her lips along scars, moving lower and lower until the tip of her tongue touched the tip of—

"What's gotten into you?" he asked hoarsely, his hips rising to meet her.

"You. Just you. Three weeks of sleeping beside you. Wanting. Needing. I forget why we weren't doing this all along." She heard him suck in a deep breath as she took him inside her mouth and cherished him, thrilled at his guttural response, at the way his fingers dug into her scalp. He tried to pull her up, but she wouldn't let him, treating him—and herself—to the absolute pleasure of it all. She loved him. Had head-over-heels-forever fallen in love with him. Of all the disastrous, wondrous things to have happened....

Tony dragged her up and switched their positions. He kissed her back just as thoroughly, wondering at her mood and actions. While she'd been a partner that first time, not just a participant, this was different. Almost...desperate.

Because of that he slowed things down, undressed her like a gift, the wrapping too pretty to ruin, enjoying the way she urged him to hurry, which made him slow down even more. He peeled away her clothes, revealing the perfect temptation of her body. America's Sexpot, he thought, glad the rest of the world didn't know that about her. Glad she'd chosen *him*.

He hadn't seen this wild side of her, not to this extent. He was fascinated by it and her, and whatever was driving her. He'd barely got her undressed, barely glided his fingertips down her body once before she was climaxing. Challenged, he took her up again before she'd even come down from the first. Then he rose over her and buried himself in her heat, then he went still, absolutely still.

She made a long, low sound of pleasure, told him how good he felt, how he filled her with fire. He wanted to drag it out forever, burn the moment like a brand into his mind, but her words snapped his control. He drew back then plunged. Her legs wrapped around him tighter, higher. He drove himself to meet her demands and took everything she offered, giving everything back. Her heart pounded so hard he could feel it reverberate through her whole body, along her throat, where he pressed his lips as they climaxed together. It was the most memorable sex of his life—and that was saying something, considering their first time, almost a month ago.

The moment ebbed, satisfaction blanketing them. He tucked her close. She wrapped her arms around him and clung. Her breath heated his skin.

"Welcome home," he murmured.

Her body shook with quiet laughter. "Glad to be here."

After a minute or so passed she finally let out a long sigh. "How'd your cattle drive go?" she asked, snuggling down, toying with his chest hair, finally seeming to relax.

"Nothing out of the ordinary. We got done early."

"I noticed. I'm glad."

"How was your trip to San Francisco? Everything in order?"

"Looks good. They're ready for us." She yawned. "I didn't sleep well with you gone."

"I slept in a bedroll in a teepee with four hundred cows milling around, including a bunch of bawling calves. I think you probably did a tad better than me."

She laughed quietly. "Probably so. You must be exhausted."

"I am. We can sleep in a little, though, right? You're all done filming?"

"Done. The seamstress and tailor will be here in the morning to fit us for our wedding clothes, then will head over to your parents' ranch. If you've got time tomorrow, I'd like to go visit your mom and tell her about the wedding plans now that I've got a picture in my head of how everything is going to work."

"I can manage that." He wondered if he should tell her about the honeymoon he'd arranged. Wondered if he should tell her about his bank account. She'd seemed to worry about spending money on her when he'd bought her engagement ring. He felt as if he was cheating a little by not cluing her in, but since only one other person knew he'd made a killing in the stock market through the years…

Later, he decided. Or maybe not ever, depending on what happened between them down the line. It wasn't as if she needed a financial commitment from him. She did just fine on her own.

He'd had a prenup drawn up and needed to present it at some point soon. He was surprised she hadn't done so herself. Or maybe she had, but, like him, had kept it quiet so far.

So. He kept secrets from her. She probably kept secrets from him.

Not the greatest way to start a marriage, even a fake one. But he'd confided a lot in his first wife, and in the end been sorry about it. She'd thrown it back in his face, all the personal pain he'd shared. And then she'd left, which had been just fine at that point.

But with Maggie? This was a mature relationship, not one based on fantasies. Sort of. Would they continue to make love or would they go back to square one?

Tonight marked a turning point for them. But just which way would it turn?

He only knew he didn't want anything to change now. He was more content than he'd been in a long time, maybe ever. And contentment was hard to come by.

Chapter Twelve

"It's my gift to you," Maggie said to Sue-Ellen the next day as she was fitted for her mother-of-the-groom dress, a periwinkle organza gown with a beaded shawl. Her future sisters-in-law and their daughters had already come and gone. "I want you to feel comfortable."

"Gracious, I don't feel comfortable at all. I feel elegant. Aren't I supposed to? Like Grace Kelly." She posed. "Or maybe more like Barbara Stanwyck at the end of her career. And for you to get all of us dresses, even the granddaughters, and all the men and boys tuxes—well, it's just too much."

"Just remember the designer's name when you're asked," she said with a smile. "I'm glad we didn't waste a lot of time arguing about it. If you don't count Hoyt."

"Well, once you told him he wouldn't have to wear a bow tie, he was okay with it. He wants Tony to be proud.

We'll have to figure out someplace else to wear the fancy duds at some point."

The woman pinning her hem sat back on her heels. "Done. Thank you. It'll be at the hotel waiting for you."

Maggie thanked the seamstress for coming. As soon as Sue-Ellen had changed, the gowns were taken away.

"I think Tony will be tied up for a while. Have you seen our property yet?" Sue-Ellen asked, dressed in her usual jeans and shirt again. "Would you like to take a ride?"

"I'd love to. I've only had a quick tour by truck." Maggie wondered how Tony was doing. He'd left the women to talk, reluctantly joining his father and brothers, who were building a new mare motel, he called it.

"Good, because I already had two horses saddled," Sue-Ellen said, almost winking. "Yours is Buttercup. I wasn't about to take no for an answer."

"Yes, ma'am."

Sue-Ellen laughed. "You ever say that to anyone before?"

"No, ma'am. Never figured to, either."

"Shows you how life can change, doesn't it?"

"In a heartbeat."

They walked outside. The horses waited at the hitching post off the porch. Tony wasn't in sight.

"The men are down the hill a ways, behind the big shed," Sue-Ellen said knowingly. "You can't see them from here. We'll drop by and tell them where we're headed."

"Okay. Thanks." Since realizing—and accepting—last night that she'd fallen in love with Tony, Maggie had felt… different. Her pulse never quieted. She wanted to be next to him all the time. Then she didn't want to be around him at all. She wanted to touch him every second. Then she wanted to stay far, far away.

During breakfast he'd flat-out asked what was wrong with her. How could she answer that? Nothing was wrong. Everything was wrong.

She zeroed in on Tony as she and Sue-Ellen approached by horseback. His heels were dug into the earth as he held a bar in place while his brother Grady attached the other end of it. Cal and Hoyt worked on a crossbar. Grunts and head gestures were their form of communication.

Tony spotted them first. "Where're you two headed?"

"Your mom's going to show me where you used to swim naked."

"I never—"

Maggie laughed. "Just having fun with you, cowboy."

"I was going to say, before you interrupted—" he ambled over and ran his hand down her leg "—I never got caught."

"So you'd like to think," Sue-Ellen said. "There's only a couple of good places. Hoyt and I found them, too, but sometimes we had to pull back, 'cause one of you boys was there."

"Too much information," Grady called out. "Tony, quit flirtin' and get your butt back here. I can't hold this thing forever."

"Have a good time," Tony said to Maggie, giving her leg a squeeze.

She didn't want to leave him, but she nodded and nudged her horse to get going. Sue-Ellen came alongside her. They moved along at a steady pace, not talking much.

Like Tony's, his parents' land started flat then rose. She'd learned they had to have elevation for the best grazing, a graduated terrain, and year-round access. Although it took forty-five minutes to drive from one ranch to the other, they looked similar, at least to Maggie.

"It's beautiful country," she said to Sue-Ellen, who looked out at her land with satisfaction in her eyes.

"I wouldn't want to be anywhere else. It's not an easy life, but I think I've been a good ranch wife."

Maggie had learned that term from Sadie. Being called a good ranch wife was high praise. It meant she had give and didn't whine and knew how to become a hand when necessary, and a helpmate the rest of the time. She could doctor anything her man couldn't. She was strong and didn't take to her bed unless she'd just given birth. She cooked, cleaned and managed the finances. And she earned her man's utter devotion by being all that.

"Nothing in my life has prepared me for that role," Maggie said honestly.

"I was the same. Oh, not famous or anything like that, but a city girl. Hoyt found me working as a file clerk in Phoenix. I'd never sat a horse. But I loved that man with all my being, and so I learned what I needed to know and found I loved it all."

"No regrets?"

"Nope. I don't mean that everything's been perfect all the time. Every path has a few puddles, after all, but in the grand scheme of things, it's been a good life. Probably lived as long and healthy as I have because I always worked hard. I'm proud of my children, tickled pink with my grandchildren. I hope the good Lord takes me and Hoyt together, and that's a fact. And it'll be easy to go knowing that Cal and Grady will keep the place going, Tony's got his own, and Mary Beth's secure."

Maggie pondered Sue-Ellen's words. Her grandparents had been that devoted to each other and had gotten their wish, dying only a week apart.

"I read that your parents and brother died in a car accident," Sue-Ellen said.

"I was ten. I remember how much fun we had together, and my mom always coming to the set with me, which can often be a problem. But the production people liked her. She had a way about her that led to things getting done in a way that was satisfactory to her without alienating anyone."

A memory jumped out at Maggie, one she'd set aside for years. "I remember my first day back on set after the funeral. Everyone cried. Everyone. We ended up not working that day but having a memorial of our own. People told stories, some of them pretty funny, things I hadn't known about her. The series only lasted to the end of that season, then I took two years off from television and did a couple of movies."

"Your grandparents raised you."

She nodded. "As an adult I can look back and see how much they sacrificed for me. They were uncomplicated people who uprooted themselves from Georgia to move to Hollywood so that I could keep working." Maggie went quiet for a minute, the memories sharp, as she let her horse follow Sue-Ellen's up a narrow trail then back into the open. "Once I was grown and living in my own house, they moved back to Georgia, but the high standards my grandmother held me to stuck with me. Everything I did, I was aware of her voice in my head, saying it was right or wrong. 'What would Gram think?' became my first question."

"I don't know for sure what I thought when Tony said he was marrying you," Sue-Ellen said, "but you are more than I expected. He's happy, and that's what matters most to me, but you're a gem on your own."

Maggie went silent. Guilt heaped upon guilt. Her grandmother would be very disappointed. To marry for the sake of appearances? Not good. Not right.

But it wasn't without love, she told herself. She did love him. She just couldn't tell him that or he might change his mind—and she needed time to get him to love her back.

All she could do was try to show him she loved him before he pulled the plug on the marriage weeks or months down the road, whenever he decided to end it.

Tony kept an eye toward the east and Maggie's return. He wondered what she and his mother were talking about for so long, didn't understand how women could keep up a running dialogue for hours. Finally they appeared, looking easy with each other. He sought his mother's eyes first, trying to see anything different there, to know if Maggie had said things she shouldn't have, but his mother only smiled and gave him an unobtrusive thumbs-up.

He shifted his gaze to Maggie, who did look at him differently. But then she'd been different since she got home from San Francisco last night and come at him like a wild creature, all hot and needy. They hadn't talked about it this morning. Not one word. He didn't know what to make of that—or her.

"Lunch'll be ready in thirty minutes," Sue-Ellen said to the group at large.

"We'll be done here by then," Tony said. "Don't go to any trouble for Maggie and me. We'll be heading out."

"Well, since my daughters-in-law brought lunch to the house, I can't say it'd be any trouble, son. And you gotta eat."

He looked to Maggie, who raised her brows and smiled. He'd come to the conclusion that she was a lot more comfortable around his family than he was.

"Okay. We'll leave right after, though. Got some things to do at home." Like make love to her in the broad daylight, something he hadn't done before. Maybe they could just slip into the shower together and soap each other up—

"Meantime, there's this to finish," his father said as the women rode their horses into the barn.

"I remember being that hot to trot," Tony's brother Cal said as they installed the last gate. He'd been married twenty-five years. "Get it while you can," he said, elbowing Tony. "Before they're too tired."

"Maggie'll never get tired," Grady said, grinning broadly. "She'll be off makin' millions makin' movies. Must be nice, livin' the life of Riley like that, eh, brother?"

Tony would've taken it in jest except that his father added, "Probably wouldn't make a good ranch wife, anyway."

Tony went ramrod straight. "You don't know her well enough to know that."

"You ever looked at her hands? Bet she's never picked up a shovel."

"So what? She works hard at what she does. I thought you liked her." *Better than me, your own son.*

"I was just sayin'." Hoyt's jaw went rigid. "You got to admit, it's a leap for a woman like that."

"You have no idea what that woman is made of. You think I'd choose someone frivolous?"

"You have in the past."

Tony handed his wrench to Grady. He needed to get away before he said something that should come in private, whenever their big showdown happened. And it would happen sometime.

He went straight to the barn, where Maggie was grooming the horse she'd ridden.

"Let's go," he said.

"What? Why? I need to finish with Buttercup. Plus, we're all having lunch—"

"Someone else can take over with the horse. Sorry about lunch, Mom. We'll see you later."

"I have to get my purse from the house," Maggie said, confusion on her face as she looked back and forth between mother and son.

"Fine. I'll meet you at the truck."

"What'd your father say this time?" Sue-Ellen asked after Maggie was out of sight.

"It doesn't bear repeating."

"He doesn't know how to talk to you, son. Never has."

"Well, that goes both ways." The old memory flared, from when he was twelve and he'd overheard his father—

"He loves you."

"He tolerates me. Look, Mom, let's just stop it here." What made it harder was knowing his father would end up being right when his marriage to Maggie ended, as if he wasn't man enough to keep her. The thought wore him down.

There's still time to get out.

Nope. Never. He'd never been a quitter. Wasn't starting now, either.

He got to the truck the same time as Maggie. He held the door for her, stood perfectly still as she cupped a hand to his face.

The ride to the Lucky Hand was quiet and tense.

"What happened?" Maggie asked finally as they headed up the final road to the house.

"Same ol', same ol'."

"I figure it was about me."

He debated a bit with himself before answering. "No.

It was about me. It's always about me. I've never been good enough."

"How much of that is in your head, Tony?"

He looked sharply at her. "Don't be my analyst, okay? I know what I know."

She got an annoyed look on her face, but he had no intention of explaining anything. When he pulled up by the house, she hopped out and hurried into the house. Dino wandered over before Tony could follow.

"Sadie and Leesa headed into Phoenix to shop," Dino said. "Everything okay?"

"She's ticked at me."

"Good."

"Good? Why's that?"

Dino crossed his arms. "She never gets mad, at least not in front of anyone. If she's showing you she's mad, it's healthy, I think."

"Interesting theory."

"I've been with her ten years. I know her pretty well. So, I can also tell you this—she doesn't hold on to her anger."

So if he played his cards right, he could still get lucky. Still make love to her in the daylight. Especially now that the house was empty, and she wouldn't be worrying about anyone hearing them.

Tony clapped Dino on the shoulder. "Thanks."

"You planning on going anywhere else today?"

"Nothing on the agenda. We'll probably take a nap." He started up the stairs.

"I'll see you aren't disturbed."

Tony glanced back as he opened the door, hearing a touch of humor in Dino's voice, but he'd turned away.

Tony steeled himself for battle. She was a woman, after all, and would want to "fix" things, get him to see his father's point of view or something.

He didn't find her in the kitchen. She wasn't in the bedroom, either. He headed into the master bath and found her bare naked next to the shower. She leaned into it and turned on the faucets.

"Took you long enough, cowboy."

She was every fantasy he'd ever had come to life. She didn't move but just watched him undress, dropping his filthy clothes in a heap on the floor then approaching her, aware of his sweat and dirt. Dino knew her well. She'd left her anger behind—or was delaying further discussion.

"I guess you're happy to see me," she said pertly.

"Always."

"I've noticed. I'm flattered."

"Sadie and Leesa are gone for the day."

Her brows rose. "Are they?"

He nodded. They came body to body. "You can make all the noise you want," he said, dragging his lips along her jaw, up to the perfect shell of her ear. "I know you were holdin' back last night."

She gasped a little as he tickled her ear with his tongue. "How would you know that?"

"Those teeth marks you left in my shoulder." He moved her into the shower with him, reached for the bar of soap. "You still mad at me?" he asked.

"Yes."

"Good."

"Good?"

He ran the bar over her breasts. "Yeah. It'll make

things even more intense." He thumbed soap around her hard nipples.

She closed her eyes and groaned…

It was the beginning of a long, glorious afternoon.

Chapter Thirteen

When Tony awoke the next morning, Maggie was gone. He looked at the clock—5:25—and noticed that no lights were on in the bathroom. He climbed out of bed, headed for the living room then remembered he needed to wear something, since Leesa was in the house.

He pulled on his jeans. Barefoot he made his way through the living room into the kitchen, the smell of fresh coffee drawing him, but that room was empty, too.

Where was she?

He poured a cup then went out on his front porch, noting that the door was unlocked. No Maggie there, either.

He stepped off the porch and went around the side of the house to Dino's RV. The door swung open before he knocked. Dino was fully dressed.

"Have you seen Maggie?" Tony asked. He'd never been

witness to anyone going into full-alert mode like Dino did right then.

He hurried down the stairs and looked around. "You lost her?"

"I wouldn't go that far. She's not in the house, but she made a fresh pot of coffee. She probably went for a walk."

"Aren't you going to go look for her?"

"Not sure I should," Tony countered. "Apparently she wants to be alone." *Or she would've awakened me and told me she was going—or invited me to come along.*

Leesa stuck her head out the guest-room window. "What's going on?"

"Maggie's missing," Dino answered.

"What? When? How?"

"She's not missing, exactly," Tony said, almost laughing. "She's just not in the house. I figure she's out for a walk."

"Well, there's nothing else to do in this place, so you're probably right," Leesa said with a yawn.

Tony had been wondering how Leesa was dealing with living so far from the city. He knew she didn't have much to do now that filming was over. She sounded bored. "I'll get dressed and see if I can catch up with her," Tony said.

"I'll go, too," Dino added.

"And *I'm* going back to bed." Leesa shut her window.

A few minutes later, Tony and Dino met out front, debated about whether to drive or walk, then set out on foot down the hill toward the barn and other outbuildings. Dino had already contacted his men, who roamed the land by Jeep, and no one had seen her.

Tony refused to worry.

They got within sight of the stables, could hear someone singing. Sort of. "Who's that?" Tony asked, afraid of the answer.

"Your lovely bride-to-be."

"No wonder she's never done any musicals."

Dino laughed, but Tony could tell he was relieved. So was Tony, although more annoyed than relieved.

"You can go back," Tony said.

Dino gave him a curious look but said nothing. He turned away and headed up the hill. Tony continued on to the stables, following her voice. She was messing up the lyrics so much he wasn't even sure which song she was singing, some odd combination of "Home on the Range" and "She'll Be Coming 'Round the Mountain."

"What are you doing?" he asked from the open doorway.

She whirled around. Her cheeks were flushed already, but he thought they deepened in color. "Singing."

It wasn't what he'd meant, but he went with it. "I take exception to that claim."

She leaned against her stall-fork handle. "So I've been told. I didn't think the horses would mind."

He came up to her, plucked a piece of straw from her hair, then another. She looked as if she'd rolled out of bed and come directly to the stables. "What's your natural hair color?" he asked.

"Brown, but with a little more gold than the red it is now."

"Will you have to change it for your next role?"

"I don't know yet. Do you mind this color? I hadn't thought I'd change it for the wedding."

"It's fine."

"Fine? Now *there's* a high compliment."

"You're beautiful. I've told you that. What color your hair is doesn't change that." He looked around, checking out the horses, who didn't look any worse for wear having listened to her singing, a sound that must've seemed strange to them. "You're up early, Margaret."

"Couldn't sleep."

"How come?"

"I don't know. I heard Sadie come in, and I got out of bed to see how she was feeling, because yesterday she wasn't well."

It was the first he'd heard of it. "What's wrong with her?"

"Flu, maybe. Butch is taking her to her obstetrician today. He needs to be sure she can fly to San Francisco tomorrow. Anyway, I sent her back to bed. I told her I'd take care of the meals today."

"Yeah? What does that mean? That you'll draft Dino or Leesa to take over?"

She swatted at him. "Show up at seven o'clock and find out."

"Wouldn't miss it." He gestured toward the stalls. "So, what's with the mucking?"

"Felt the urge."

"You felt the urge to muck stalls?" He put a hand against her forehead, and she smiled. "You know you're taking away from someone else's job, right? Someone who depends on the income?"

Color drained from her face. "No."

"Bopper. Kid from a neighboring ranch. He shows up at six. Takes care of things then heads to school."

"I'm so sorry. I'll make sure to be here so I can apologize. I was just trying to be helpful."

"Helpful," he repeated thoughtfully. "Actually, you didn't take away any work from him, since we muck the stuff into a wheelbarrow, not onto the ground. Makes it easier to haul it over to the compost heap. He'll still have to load the wheelbarrow."

She frowned but stayed silent. Tony looked around the stables, debating what to say, whether to tell her what was on his mind, then decided he would. "Why'd you leave without telling me? We had this discussion before. You promised you wouldn't do that again. Even Dino didn't know you'd gone."

"I wanted you to sleep in. And just how far do you think I would—or could—go?"

"You sound irritated."

"Look, Tony, I was just trying to be helpful. Is there something wrong with that?"

Her defensive tone gave him pause. What was really going on? "Nothing, except that we're a pretty smooth-running operation. There aren't a lot of jobs that need tending." At least, not ones she could physically handle, more along the lines of tearing down and building structures, rerunning water lines or some such business. "Are you bored now that you're not working? I realize you're not in your own place, with friends around. Figure it's hard on you."

She shook her head. "It's not. I'm enjoying the break and the different way of life. I'm trying—" She stopped, turned away, taking her stall fork with her.

"Trying what?"

"To be a good ranch wife," she muttered, hanging the tool up on the wall where it belonged.

He followed. "Did my father say something to you?"

She faced him, her arms crossed. "No. Is that what ticked you off yesterday? Did he criticize me?"

"Nothing he says matters to me."

"That's such a lie, Tony. What he says matters way too much to you."

Ice slithered through him like a deadly rattler. "When did you become the expert on my relationship with my father?"

"I listen. I observe." She put her hand on his arm.

He sloughed it off, moved back a little. "I don't want to talk about it."

"Okay."

"But this business about being a good ranch wife? It has nothing to do with the work you do on the ranch."

"That's not what I heard."

"It counts, but it's the least important. You already have a job. You bring in an income. That also matters, since ranching doesn't turn much profit. The problem you would run up against—if you were going to truly be a ranch wife, not just filling the position temporarily—is fitting in. A good ranch wife's social life is church on Sunday morning and the occasional potluck dinner followed by horseshoes. These folks around here have known each other all their lives, and in a lot of cases are related to one another, a lot by marriage. Cracking that circle can be tough."

She looked defeated. He couldn't stand that. "I would face the same thing with your circle, darlin'. I wouldn't fit in. Not by a long shot."

"I don't think it's a matter of you fitting in. You'd hold your own anywhere. It's a matter of me not wanting you to even try. It's not your kind of world. It's barely my kind."

What was she saying? Should he read between the lines? Maybe—

"Hey, boss. Something wrong?" Bopper, a tall, lanky teen sauntered in. He tipped his hat at Maggie then realized who she was. He looked at the ground, shifted from foot to foot. "Ma'am."

"Nothing's wrong, Bopper—"

"Oh, you're Bopper!" Maggie exclaimed.

That brought the boy's head up in a hurry.

"I'm so *sorry*," she said, then gestured to the heap of manure she'd created. "I did some of your work this morning. I didn't realize I shouldn't, and maybe I even made your job worse. You'll still get paid in full, no matter what. Or more, if it takes you longer."

Tony laughed quietly. She really was something else. As if he wouldn't pay the boy what he was due.

"Don't you need to start fixing breakfast?" he asked her, wanting to get her away so that Bopper wouldn't end up late to school. It was obvious the teenager wasn't going to do anything but stare at Maggie.

"Breakfast is under control," she said, "but I could use a shower." She extended her hand to Bopper. "It was nice meeting you. I hope I didn't make you late."

"Yes, ma'am. I mean, no, ma'am." He shook Maggie's hand. "I'll be just fine."

Tony and Maggie turned to leave.

"Ma'am? Would you mind if I took a picture with you? My friends aren't gonna believe it." He passed his cell phone to Tony and showed him which button to push.

Maggie slipped her arm through Bopper's, angling her head toward him. Tony was impressed and a little amazed that she didn't at least fluff her hair first. She wore no makeup, either, yet she let her picture be taken.

"Thanks," Bopper said, his grin wide as he tucked the phone in his pocket again. "Thanks a lot."

"I'll be seeing you around, I'm sure," she said, then moved out of the stables with Tony. They walked up the hill to the house. "Nice boy," she said.

"I suppose you're used to males getting all tongue-tied and flustered around you, especially boys like Bopper."

"A little. Even big boys. Not you, though."

"I'm not a boy."

"I did happen to notice that manly detail, cowboy."

They walked without talking after that. He wondered at her silence, unusual for her.

"So, what's for breakfast?" he asked.

"French toast, ham, melon and orange juice."

"Sounds great." And uncomplicated, since French toast was something even he could make. "Want help fixing it?"

"No, thanks."

More walking, more silence. "Leesa's got cabin fever," he said.

"I know. I don't know what to do about it. I can't let her leave, not before the wedding, anyway. She's handling a lot of the details regarding all the guests."

"And with my family. She's very efficient."

"You can say that again. I don't want to lose her, so I might just let her have the run of the Malibu house and we'll work by phone until… Well, you know."

Until the marriage is ended. The timing of which they'd agreed was his decision. "You're headed to New York in a few weeks."

"Which will make her very happy. She loves the city."

He couldn't put his finger on it, but there was something off with her. She was too subdued. Postfilming letdown? Prewedding calm before the storm?

The fact he didn't know the answer made him realize how little he knew her, even after almost a month. He'd learned what she liked in bed. She'd told him she ate any kind of food except organ meat. He'd seen for himself that she didn't watch horror movies unless a friend had a role in it. Even then she watched with her hands over her eyes most of the time.

He knew, too, that she wanted a family of her own, that she'd taken to his family and was content to spend time with them. So content, in fact, that he wondered if it was a major part of his appeal to her.

"You're quiet this morning," he finally said, curiosity getting the better of him.

She shrugged and smiled at the same time.

"Not going to tell me why?" he asked.

She looked straight ahead. He followed her line of vision, spotting Dino waiting outside his RV just as she looped her arm through his and leaned her head against his shoulder, obviously for Dino's benefit.

"There's no reason in particular," she said. "I'm enjoying the morning here on your ranch. It's been a spiritual highlight of my life."

"Spiritual? You love the smell of manure in the morning, Margaret?"

She grinned. "It doesn't smell like manure. Well, outside the stables it doesn't, anyway. The air here is so… crisp and clean. The sky is so incredibly blue. It touches me deep inside."

Also aware of their audience, Tony kissed her head as he considered how well they'd been playing house together. He was a realistic man, knew she didn't belong on the Lucky Hand. He was glad she was enjoying herself and the novelty of her situation, but the isolation would get to her at some point, probably sooner than later, and he would put an end to the marriage…

Not until he got tired of her, however, which was bound

to happen. Every relationship got stale. Although now that they were having sex, it could take a while longer.

They reached the house. She claimed the shower. He didn't argue, figuring she had to get busy with breakfast, but he leaned against the bathroom sink and watched her through the glass enclosure, talking to her so that she thought he had a reason to be there. Otherwise it would just seem…voyeuristic, even though he had every right to be there.

"You sure you don't want help in the kitchen?" he asked, passing her a towel as she opened the shower door.

"Thanks. And no thanks."

He grabbed another towel and dried her back.

"What are you, my lady's maid?" she asked, smiling in the mirror at him.

He met her gaze. "If we had time I'd lick all the water off."

Her eyes got bright. "I could probably use another shower after I'm done putting breakfast on the table."

"You think it'll be that strenuous?"

"Oh, I'm sure of it."

The thought of running his tongue over her whole body made him ache with need. "You've got yourself a date."

When he emerged from his own shower later she was gone. He dressed and wandered to the kitchen, noticing that the dining-room table was set for six.

He didn't know what he'd expected. Chaos, perhaps? Clutter, at least. But the kitchen was orderly, with nothing on the counter but a pitcher of orange juice. He smelled fresh coffee, heard the distinctive sound signifying it was almost done dripping.

She leaned her elbows against the counter and smiled at him as he opened the oven door.

"There's French toast and ham in here," he said, unable to hide his shock.

"Just as I said."

"How'd you do that? Oh, I know. Sadie cooked it at her house and Butch brought it over."

"No, but you're warm. Breakfast is compliments of the executive chef of the Desert Canyon Resort and Spa. So are lunch and dinner, which are in the refrigerator, ready to serve and/or reheat."

"You cheated."

"How so? I said I was taking care of breakfast. I did."

"You made a phone call."

"But I thought of it. And I set the table. Found platters. Tracked down maple syrup." She was grinning by now.

"What's for lunch?"

"Sandwiches and potato salad."

"And dinner?"

"Something incredible, I'm sure. It's all packaged up."

"You don't know what it is, Margaret? I could've barbecued steaks."

"I know that. This was more fun. I told them to surprise me."

She was proud of herself, he realized, like this was some kind of accomplishment. Just like mucking the stalls. Had she really done so little for herself before?

He decided to change the subject. "So, who's joining us for breakfast?"

"Dino and Leesa. Butch and Sadie."

"Sadie's feeling okay?"

"She says she's better. I'm fixing her dry toast, then she'll see how she does. She's not comfortable having me wait on her, I can tell you that."

"No surprise there."

Leesa showed up, fresh from a shower, her hair still wet. Dino came through the kitchen door, looking bewildered and out of his element, followed immediately by Butch and Sadie.

Tony enjoyed watching Maggie pamper her guests. Her eyes lit with pleasure throughout serving them all and then sitting to eat with them. Conversation flowed freely—except from Dino—then Butch and Sadie left for her doctor's appointment, Dino slipped out and Leesa asked if she could take the SUV into Phoenix for the day.

Tony loaded the dishwasher, and Maggie tidied up. Then they were done and alone.

She seemed nervous. He wondered why.

"I believe we have a date," he said, hooking his arm around her waist and pulling her close.

"You don't have work to do?"

Meaning? Was she trying to avoid him? What was going on with her? "Not until Butch gets back. You change your mind? Lost the mood?" Was it the beginning of the end for them? "Slave too hard over a hot stove?" he added, hoping to make her smile.

She put her hands along his face and went up on tiptoe. Then she kissed him, almost desperately. He didn't push her for an answer but swept her into his arms and carried her to his room, where he enjoyed every inch of her…

Even if a voice in his head kept reminding him that something had changed with her. And in his experience change was rarely good.

Chapter Fourteen

The day before the wedding, Maggie awakened early and watched Tony sleep. She struggled not to comb his hair back with her fingers so that she could see his face better. *I love you, cowboy.* The words stayed trapped in her head, echoing loudly, haunting and taunting.

That's the price you pay for messing with the sacred institution of marriage.

She hadn't taken her attraction to him seriously in the beginning. She'd been looking for a solution to her problems, and Tony had been standing there, a sexy and willing solution. At the time, she hadn't considered she wouldn't want to end the marriage at some point, or how much she'd asked of him.

He was the same as he'd been from the moment she'd met him—patient, independent, sexy—and that was the problem. He hadn't changed, while she was a different person. Loving him had changed her. She'd fallen for him fast, but she hadn't trusted her feelings, not after doing the same with Scott.

But not like this. Not with the consuming need to be with Tony all the time, to want to please him, to want to fit into his world, something that not only didn't seem to matter to him, but probably wouldn't be possible, anyway.

Maggie rolled onto her back and stared at the ceiling. How could she fit in here? Who would give her a chance? Even his father didn't think she could. She wanted not to have to depend on so many other people in her life to get her through. She wanted to do more for herself. She'd tried—in the stable and taking care of the meals yesterday.

She just hadn't had enough time to prove herself to Tony, to get him to fall in love with her.

Plus, there was his family to consider, and his already tenuous relationship with his father, who would be proven right, in Tony's mind anyway, when the marriage ended. His mother and everyone else would hate her.

Somehow she'd fallen in love with them, too, especially his mother, who always had hugs to spare, who loved Tony, who would be so disappointed in both of them.

It seemed like a worse lie than their original plan. At least with that, they both knew the marriage would end. Now she didn't want it to end. Ever.

How could she marry him knowing she didn't want a divorce? She didn't want to do that to him, to see him hurt in his family's eyes, to be the subject of tabloid stories that would haunt him for a long time.

She thought she'd been driven by a need for family and stability, but she could see now that it was balance she was seeking. Not career or family, but both, with career taking a backseat most of the time.

Now what? She closed her eyes, as tears welled. She wanted him. Wanted to marry him and be his wife forever—for real. To have his babies. To escape Hollywood, to work now and then only on projects that mattered to her.

She'd earned enough money for a lifetime. Now she wanted to have a life.

But she didn't want to marry him unless he loved her— *I-do-forever* loved her. Didn't want to do that to him.

If she canceled the wedding, she'd be the subject of a bigger scandal than before, because people would really question her sanity. Had Maggie McShane gone over the deep end? Was she cracking up? Had America's sweetheart been a façade?

That kind of false speculation would hurt, but she could weather that. And if not? Well, the punishment should fit the crime.

She'd brought it all on herself.

And now she knew she couldn't put it on Tony now.

What she'd needed was time. She'd run out of time. Yet that same amount of time had made her a much stronger woman, too. She could face anything now. Her grandmother would be so proud.

"You're up before the roosters." Tony's voice drifted over her, rough with sleep.

She crowed softly, then stretched and yawned, dragging her hands along her face to dry the tears that had dripped into her hair.

"I thought we didn't have to head to the airport until noon," he said, sliding an arm over her waist.

"You're right. Airport at noon. Rehearsal at The Taka at five. Rehearsal dinner immediately after."

He was quiet for a few beats. "What's wrong?"

The tears returned. She couldn't stop them. So much for her acting skills. She couldn't even speak.

"Wedding jitters?" he asked.

"In a way."

He said nothing for a long time. "I'm guessing we should be dressed for this discussion." He rolled out of bed, grabbed his jeans, tossed her a robe.

She pulled it on then sat cross-legged on the bed. He sat at the end, his face grim. "So, what's going on?" he asked.

"I think we should call off the wedding."

Silence fell between them for a few tense seconds.

"Like hell we will."

"Tony, I—"

"No. I don't want to hear it." He left the room in great, long strides.

Stunned, she didn't move. He hadn't asked why. What person doesn't ask why? So she hadn't had a chance to tell him, either, that she loved him, that she couldn't marry him knowing she didn't want it to end, how unfair that was to him. Didn't he want to know why? She would. She would want a complete and thorough discussion, and—to know how he felt, too.

No. He wouldn't want to hear a long explanation. He'd want it short and sweet. But she had too much to explain for that.

But maybe he'd changed his mind, too? Maybe he felt different now? Should she ask him, or would that put him on the spot too much? They had an agreement. He only wanted her to honor it.

He returned, holding a legal document, tossing it and a pen on the bed in front of her. "Our lawyers have vetted the prenup. I assume you got a copy to review."

"Yes. Tony—"

"We made a deal, Maggie."

Maggie. Hearing that name from his lips was like a knife to her heart. "I need to tell you why," she said. "You need to know why."

"I don't care why. Nothing you say would make a difference."

She grasped at straws. "I'll still finance whatever you need for the ranch. You won't lose—"

"We made a *deal,*" he repeated, low and harsh. "Part of that deal was that *I* got to call off the marriage, not you. I haven't decided to do that."

She was a coward not to just tell him right now, no matter what he said. She'd never been a coward. She'd never wanted anything so much, either. Now she would have a bigger hurdle to getting him to love her.

"I'm goin' for a ride," he said, his voice tight. He started to leave, then turned back around. "I never would've thought this of you. Never."

With those words ringing in her head, she watched him leave, wondering how they were supposed to look like a couple in love and about to get married.

She could act her way through anything, but could he?

Tony stood at the bottom of the jet stairs, the last to board the chartered plane. He'd been able to avoid Maggie until now, but as soon as he got on board he would have to act like the happy groom.

Until five o'clock this morning it would've been simple.

After she'd dropped her bomb on him he'd ridden as far out as he thought his horse could handle and still have enough in him for the ride back. Tony had been angry before, hurt, too, plenty of times. He'd lived down his divorce by keeping quiet about it. Maggie was a celebrity. No way would it be quiet.

She'd changed his life with the deal they'd made. He never reneged on a deal, and he wouldn't let her, either.

He'd thought they'd reached some kind of accord, had gone from resisting each other to not being able to get enough of each other, at least in bed. He'd been looking forward to what was ahead.

Now he either had to fake his way through the next couple of days or call it off.

Call it off. Those words had been shouting at him for hours, even though she'd signed the prenup and left it on his desk without comment.

Conversation and laughter drifted from inside the plane, filled to the brim with his family and a few friends. The women in his family were all aflutter at the star treatment. His nieces and nephews were boisterous, their excitement uncontained at the novelty of the whole thing. His father had looked into his eyes for a few long seconds then climbed the stairs, while his mother hugged him, her smile lighting up her face.

Too many people would be disappointed if the wedding didn't happen, even the hotel people, Maggie's friends, to whom she'd promised the PR event of the year.

He'd imagined it all so much differently.

"Mr. Young?"

Tony came to attention after the pilot called out from the top of the stairway.

"By my count we're all boarded except you, sir."

Tony took the stairs. He scouted the interior, saw the grins on everyone's faces. Saw, too, the empty seat next to Maggie. The only empty seat.

To hell with it. If she could act normal, so could he.

He moved down the aisle and sat beside her without looking at her face. When the plane began to taxi, he took her hand. He felt her go limp, her head coming to rest against his shoulder.

"Thank you," she whispered, her voice shaky.

"I'm doing this for all of them, not you," he fired back.

"I'll make it up to you."

"I don't want anything from you—" *Margaret.* He'd almost called her Margaret. "But we're going through with this. And everyone will see we're a loving couple, happy to get hitched. Got it?"

"Yes."

"Okay, then." He cupped her face, drawing it up so he could kiss her, only a bit of a kiss, something acceptable for public viewing, just as the plane left the ground. He should have been soaring, too.

He wasn't.

Chapter Fifteen

Through the limo window, Maggie saw her publicist standing by the revolving door of the hotel parking entrance. Three limos in succession pulled in, and Garnet hurried forward, a photographer at her side. Photos were snapped as they exited the car, walked to the entrance and stepped inside.

Maggie glanced at Tony, but his hat obscured his face. He'd have to take it off once they got inside, though, so she would have a better idea of how he was doing.

He'd been attentive on the plane, although it was all surface. Mostly it had been one big party, raucous and rowdy and a lot of fun. The two-hour trip seemed like fifteen minutes.

Everyone gawked at the incredible hotel lobby, elegant, sleek and glitteringly new.

Grady found his voice first. "You sure do know how to

pick 'em, brother. She may be ugly and the least talented person on earth, but she's got connections." He clapped Tony on the shoulder as he grinned at Maggie.

He'd insulted her. She'd been accepted. It was all she could do not to drop to her knees and bawl. Instead she hugged Grady, unable to think up any witty comeback, then she met Tony's gaze—his unreadable gaze.

"Good afternoon, everyone," a woman just outside the huge circle of people said. "My name is Andrea Clare, and I'm the wedding planner. Welcome to The Taka San Francisco. Those of you involved directly in the wedding will need to be in the grand ballroom by five o'clock for rehearsal. Then dinner will be served after to all of you at six. Each family has a staff member assigned to assist you in getting to their room. Please head to the registration desk. We have a full crew waiting. You'll be given a sheet with your instructions and a map of the hotel, but if you have any questions, please call the front desk or me personally."

The group scattered, conversation picking up again right away. Andrea approached Maggie and Tony. "Your bags are already in your rooms. I'll take you to them."

"Them?" Maggie asked.

"I assumed you'd want to keep to tradition and not see each other tomorrow before the wedding, hence the separate rooms," Andrea said. "But I can have Mr. Young's luggage moved to your suite, if you like."

"No," Tony said. "We'll keep to tradition."

Maggie figured he was relieved. They just had to make it through the rehearsal dinner, then they wouldn't have to see each other before the ceremony tomorrow. After that? Well, after that, who knew? A surprise honeymoon had been alluded to by Dino but not confirmed by Tony. Maybe he'd changed his mind. She wouldn't blame him.

"Your guests have been checking in throughout the day, Ms. McShane. We're set up for three hundred and about the equivalent in media." She grinned. "Garnet's in charge of *them,* thank goodness. Do you have any questions?"

"Were the gowns and tuxes delivered?"

"Yesterday. You and your assistant need to double-check that everything is in order, but I've been working from a master list and twenty supplemental ones addressing each contingency. I think everything is covered."

"Thank you so much for all your hard work. I'm sure it'll be a wedding to remember," Maggie said. Tony had been standing slightly apart from her, the same as he'd been in all his family photos while growing up. Part of the group, while also separate. It hurt that she'd wounded him to that point of regression.

How could she change it? What could she say?

"If you'll follow me, then," Andrea said. "You're on the top floor, Ms. McShane, and you're one below, Mr. Young. In your rooms you'll find a list with all your guests' names and room numbers. Your bars are fully stocked, as well as your refrigerators. And, of course, anything you want, you need only give the concierge or room service a call."

They checked out Tony's suite first, with its elegant luxury and commanding view of the city. He barely reacted, except to peer out the window, then they headed to Maggie's suite, which she'd seen the week before, and which was everything Tony's was and then some.

Andrea left after reminding them of the rehearsal in half an hour. It was the first they'd been alone together since early that morning. He wandered to the window. She didn't follow.

She realized how off-kilter she'd been all day with him angry at her. With Tony she'd found that elusive balance she'd been searching for. All her life she'd been adaptable, had been forced to be. Her life was one of constant change—new film, new location, new living space, new coworkers, new boss. She'd gotten so tired of it, had wondered what it would be like to have a routine she could count on most of the time. With Tony she'd seen she could have that routine, too.

The opposite would be much harder to accomplish. For any man to fit into her world would be asking a lot, and a man like Tony, who was successful in his own right, wouldn't dazzle in comparison to the limelight she occupied. Nor would he want to. And she wouldn't want to be apart from him, either.

So, really then, what were their chances of making it, even before this current issue between them?

During the plane trip, with all the noise and activity around her, she'd been struck by the realization of why she'd allowed herself to be the villain in the breakup with Scott— she'd wanted Tony from the minute they started dancing in the Red Rock Saloon. And when he'd taken charge during all that followed, she'd trusted him instantly. So she'd let herself take the hit with the media and the fans because she wanted Tony. Trusted him. Believed in him. Period.

She hadn't been forced to propose marriage to him. It hadn't been her only option. She hadn't been just keeping her word with Jenny to have her wedding at The Taka, and she hadn't been just saving face for herself, either.

She'd wanted Tony Young for her own.

"I should go change for the rehearsal," Tony said into the long silence.

She nodded. Too many revelations bombarded her, but mostly that she'd fallen in love with him at first sight, and now she'd blown it. Getting back what they had would be a maybe-insurmountable uphill battle.

He got as far as the door then turned around. "I was afraid all this wedding stuff would be too much. Too fancy," he said. "It's just classy. I should've expected that."

"Honestly, I had no hand in it. Or very little, anyway."

"You did. You may not recognize it, but you did. And my family will never forget this."

"It's been great watching them have so much fun." But she would be taken out of the family photo albums at some point, just like Tony's ex. As a family, they circled the wagons around their own.

She wanted that for herself. They would circle them for her, too, if things turned out differently.

Her heart ached. She tried to smile at Tony as he waited in silence by the door.

Finally he just left without another word. Then before the door shut, Leesa came flying in.

"It's about time, Mags. I've got a whole list of things to hash out with you. I thought he'd never leave."

And I'm afraid he will...

As the rehearsal dinner wound down, Maggie was startled when Tony laid a hand on hers on top of the table and leaned close. "The boys are taking me out for a while," he said.

Maggie glanced past him, to where Cal and Grady were grinning. She got it—a bachelor party. "Have fun," she said, shaking a be-careful finger at his brothers. "Is Butch going, too?"

"It was his idea. Something about the best man getting

the groom drunk being part of his job responsibility. How about you? Any plans for champagne and a stripper with the girls?"

"Can't escape it. Leesa used the maid-of-honor excuse to force me, too. She's off gathering up a few friends."

"Okay, then, you have fun, too."

"Thanks. I'm not sure how we're going to get out of the hotel without the paparazzi following."

"Well, don't do anything you don't want photographed."

After a long pause she took a chance and said, "It turned out for me okay the last time."

His lips thinned. "You're a very confusing woman, Maggie McShane."

His words gave her hope. She accepted a brief kiss goodbye, almost twisted her fingers into his shirt to keep him there, then smiled at the antics of his brothers as they dragged him off. "No hangovers," she called out to them.

"No promises," Grady called back.

The room was almost empty. Most people had decided to go out on the town, to see the beautiful city of San Francisco while they had the chance. Maggie walked to where Hoyt and Sue-Ellen were just getting up from their table. "Are you going carousing, too?" she asked.

"We haven't decided yet," Sue-Ellen said. "Would you mind coming to our room for a few minutes, though? I've got something I'd like to show you. Unless you've got plans?"

"I'm waiting for Leesa's signal. I've got time. Regardless, I would make time." She smiled and fell in step beside them. She and Sue-Ellen talked about the hotel and the beauty of the ballroom and how wonderful the food was. Hoyt kept his thoughts to himself, not interjecting a comment. Maggie should be used to it by now, but she still found it unnerving at times, not knowing how he felt about things. About her.

The first time they'd met he'd seemed to approve of her. Then came the day that Tony felt his father had criticized her—or whatever had happened there. She wished she knew which way Hoyt felt.

When they reached the suite, situated on the same floor as Tony's, Sue-Ellen slipped into the bedroom.

"Tony told me you've never been here," Maggie said to Hoyt as he stood looking at the view, a universal pull. The sun was setting.

"Been to Las Vegas once. That's as far north—and west—as I've been."

"Pretty amazing, isn't it?"

"Lot of people. Lot of cars. Lot of buildings. People in a rush."

"True. It doesn't rival what you've got, but as a change of pace, it's okay, don't you think?"

He eyed her. "Girl, you sure can be diplomatic."

Maggie laughed. "I'm trying."

Sue-Ellen joined them, carrying a small, flat package, wrapped prettily, with a glittery white bow. She passed it to Maggie.

"This belonged to my great-great-grandmother. If you don't have something borrowed, I'd be pleased if you would borrow this."

The box held a dainty white handkerchief with tatted edges and the monogram ESH embroidered in one corner.

"Her name was Elizabeth Starbuck Hussey," Sue-Ellen said. "She and my great-great-grandfather settled in northern Arizona in the early 1870s. I gather she was a tough cookie. Probably had to be. But I always loved her name, and treasured the only physical possession that was left of hers—that hankie."

Maggie was touched. "I'll take very good care of it. Thank you so much for letting me use it."

"It must be hard for you without your mom or grandma here with you. I know you don't need me imparting what-will-happen-on-your-wedding-night wisdom to you," she said with a wink. "But I want you to know you can come to me. I'll do my best to fill in for the women who aren't here anymore. I've come to love you already."

Maggie went into Sue-Ellen's open arms and cried, the tension of the day finally reaching the breaking point. She could blame the tears on missing her mother and grand-mother, or the exquisite acceptance by this beautiful woman to try to take their place. Both were true, after all.

"Thank you so much," she said into Sue-Ellen's shoulder. "I've come to love you, too. All of you. You're the family I've been waiting for."

"You make Tony happy, and that counts for a lot with us." She moved back a little and brushed Maggie's hair from her face. "Don't wait too long to give us a new grand-baby, okay? Hoyt and I aren't getting any younger."

Hoyt made a sound behind her. "Oh, hush up, husband. It's the truth. What's wrong with saying it?"

Hoyt shoved a box of tissues at Maggie. She did her best to staunch the tears that didn't want to stop completely.

"Here," Hoyt said, holding out his hand.

She put hers out and he dropped a penny into it.

"For your shoe, for good luck. Newly minted."

Maggie shifted to Hoyt's arms, felt him pat her awkwardly, which finally turned off her waterworks. She was smiling when she moved back. "Thank you, Hoyt. I'll treasure it."

He gave his wife a quick look. "You can call me Dad, if it falls off your tongue easily enough. If not, Hoyt's fine, too."

The weight just kept piling up on Maggie's shoulders.

Tony glanced around the bar, one about as opposite as possible from the Red Rock Saloon. The music was jazz, the clientele wore clothes he would consider dress-up but probably worked well for casual Friday in an office here.

As bachelor parties went, it was a tame one. There was some drinking, of course. That was traditional. But none of them was interested in watching a stripper gyrate as she stared off into oblivion. Been there, done that. Lost its appeal long ago.

If things were normal he'd be on his cell phone with Maggie now and then, checking out what she was doing, listening to her tell a good story about it. He left his phone in his pocket. Butch was making calls, but since his wife was pregnant, that was understandable. Sadie relayed where they were and how awesome—her word—it was to walk into a place and have everyone look at her because of Maggie and wonder if Sadie was famous, too.

Dino was with them. Tony could only smile about that. Seven women and Dino, partying their way through the city.

After watching Maggie's trying-hard-to-be-happy face all day, he'd come to wish he'd let her have her say this morning. He should've let her tell him why she wanted to call it off, because it sure didn't seem like that was what she wanted. There was only so much she could fake. After all, this wasn't a role she was playing. It was her life.

"Hey," Grady said, jabbing an elbow into Tony's side, then aiming his beer bottle at the television. "Take a gander."

It was Scott Gibson, being interviewed by one of the TV entertainment programs. Even if the sound had been turned up to maximum they couldn't have heard it over the din in the bar, but the captioning was turned on.

"So, tomorrow would've been your wedding day," the reporter asked, the words flashing on the screen.

Scott put a hand to his chest and smiled sadly. "You had to remind me."

"I was going to ask how you felt about it, but it's obvious you're not over it yet."

"Who would be? She's one special woman. I've half a mind to show up at her wedding and object."

"Like hell you will," Tony muttered then took a long sip of his beer.

"Would you really do that?" the reporter asked, almost rubbing her hands together.

"Life's full of surprises," he said with a movie-star smile.

"Yeah, like how much it costs to replace a mouth full of teeth," Tony said.

Grady punched him in the shoulder and laughed. "How long has it been since you punched out anyone?"

"Ten years, probably. Hell, it made my reputation, though. No one's really challenged me since then."

"How come you're ticked at Gibson? Should be reverse, since you stole his woman."

"Yeah, well, there's more to it than that."

"Yeah? So, it would feel kind of nice to knock Scott Gibson to the ground?"

More than nice. Great. Satisfying. He shrugged. "Won't happen. He wouldn't show up at the wedding."

"You sure about that?"

"Yep." If he did, Tony would make sure the press knew

the truth about the end of the engagement. He wouldn't get off scot-free a second time. "Let's get out of here," Tony said, standing. He needed fresh air.

"Where to?" Butch asked.

He didn't want to go back to the hotel. They had a reputation to uphold, after all, as partying men. "I don't know the city."

"How about Fisherman's Wharf?" Cal suggested.

And so the four cowboys from Arizona, wearing their best hats, vests, Wranglers and boots, ended up moseying around one of the most visited tourist spots in the whole country, watching magicians, human robots, jugglers and clowns perform their acts on the streets along the wharf, earning their living. Then they went into the Wax Museum and were stunned to come across a life-size wax Maggie, which had them laughing for the rest of the night. Even Tony grinned a few times.

Then when Sadie called Butch to say the women were back in the hotel, they figured it was time to go. Even if they hadn't gotten drunk or had a lap dance in a tawdry club, they'd stayed out later than the women. That was all that mattered.

They'd done their gender proud, Grady had announced, which set them off laughing again.

All in all, Tony thought, it had been exactly what he'd needed.

Really? Exactly what you needed?

He'd avoided thinking about the morning, and Maggie wanting to stop the wedding.

He should've let her tell him why, instead of panicking—and there was no other word for it. He was ready to marry her, wanted all the benefits that came with marriage.

What she'd said had come from out of the blue. He hadn't known how to react.

He'd been looking forward to the marriage all month. Damned if she was going to steal that from him. He'd deserved this time with her, needed it. Counted on it.

Yeah, she *had* to marry him because… He shut his eyes for a few seconds, conjuring up an image of her beautiful face. *Because* he was head over heels for her, and he needed time to show her he was a keeper.

Just a little more time.

Chapter Sixteen

They should've had a morning wedding, Tony decided. Waiting out the whole day for a five o'clock ceremony was like water torture—drips of time passing, each one more painful than the last. He'd eaten breakfast alone, watched a celebrity poker match on TV, and wished he was home, riding the range. Or at the least, out in the city, killing time by doing something, not stuck in a hotel room.

He paced, wondering what Maggie was wishing for right now. That she'd ended it when she had the chance? She'd signed the prenup, but was it just to keep the deal they'd made? To honor her word?

Was that what he wanted? For her to marry him because they made a deal?

Tony grabbed a pair of hotel-supplied binoculars and carried them to the window. He could see some of the San

Francisco Bay, dotted with sailboats and Windsurfers skimming across the white-capped surface.

He wondered how that felt, maneuvering those boards and depending on the wind to get you somewhere. It had to be easier on the bones than riding a bareback bronc. He had no desire to push his body into those contortions anymore. It was enough just getting out of bed and into the kitchen to pour coffee every day, waiting for his joints to loosen up.

Hell, he was sounding like an old man—

A knock came at his door. He didn't care who it was. Distraction would help.

He opened the door to find Cal, Grady, Butch and his father standing there. Behind them was a uniformed employee with a pushcart.

"Our wives are off getting dolled up for the wedding," Grady said, coming into the room, the others following. "We knew you'd be in a worse boat since you can't even see Maggie."

"You're right. Thanks for coming."

Grady passed some money to the room service employee before she left the room, shutting the door quietly behind her. "Well, we found out it's true, brother. A concierge can work miracles with a snap of his fingers."

From the bottom shelf of the cart he brought out a deck of cards and a double rack of poker chips. "Figured you might like to kill some time." Then from the top shelf he lifted lids off five plates holding hamburgers and thick-cut fries.

"No onions," Butch said. "I thought of that. Want that pronounce-you-man-and-wife kiss to be sweet."

"Husband and wife," Tony corrected, picking up a plate

and passing it to his father, then grabbing one for himself. "Equal partners."

Hoyt made a little sound, a kind of snort, but said nothing. Tony didn't want to get into an argument with his father today, of all days, so he left it alone.

They settled at the dining table to eat first, then turned it into a poker table. A couple of hours flew by. Hoyt had barely uttered a word the whole time, only raise, stay or fold. He had the best poker face in the world. Could've made a good living at the game, Tony thought.

"You're quiet, Butch," Tony said, dealing another hand, finally realizing his foreman had been as quiet as his father.

Butch shrugged. "One day of this was entertaining. I'm ready to be home."

Tony knew exactly what he meant.

"Yep, this celebrity business is wearisome," Cal said dramatically. "People at your beck and call, and you don't even have to pay for anything except a tip now and then. Want some food? Pick up the phone. Need extra towels, all white and fluffy and *big?* Pick up the phone. It's killing me." He grinned and started the bidding for the next round with a ten-dollar chip.

Grady tossed in his own. "I'm kinda surprised the press hasn't given you and Maggie one of those combo names, you know, mixing your first names so they don't have to say both of 'em?"

Butch added to the pot, then so did Hoyt.

Tony put in a chip, raised it ten. "I'm pretty sure you both have to be celebrities for that to work." Small blessings, he thought, that he wasn't a star himself.

"But what would yours be?" Grady asked, looking at

the ceiling and contemplating. "Let's see. Maggie. Tony. Mag…ony. Magony! Wow. That's kind of close to agony, isn't it?"

Tony smiled.

"Carrying that idea through," Cal added, "then that Scott Gibson guy she was engaged to before? They coulda been Maggott."

Grady howled. Even Hoyt cracked a smile.

"Why weren't they called that, do you suppose?" Butch asked.

"Because," Tony said, "Maggie commands a lot of respect from the media."

"Maggot," Grady repeated, chuckling. "She was destined to dump the guy. Which reminds me, I heard somewhere that he got tossed by that Gennifer rebound girl, too. Must be somethin' really wrong with the guy. Call."

They played in silence for a while. Tony raked in chips.

"Good thing we're not playing for cash," Cal said. "We'd all be contributing to your honeymoon, big time."

"Where *are* you going?" Grady asked.

"I haven't even told Maggie yet, so I'm not about to tell you," Tony answered. In fact, he was still debating about the honeymoon trip. Only Dino knew his plans—ten days in a cabin in Banff, in the Canadian Rockies, a location Dino assured him she hadn't been before. He figured there weren't a whole lot of places that qualified.

"And she's okay with that?" Cal asked. "Not knowing? Wouldn't she want to choose her steamer trunk full of clothes accordingly?"

Grady grinned. "He probably figures she won't be needing much in the way of clothing."

That's exactly what Tony had hoped for. "The fewer

people who know, the less chance of our honeymoon becoming a public spectacle."

"But, including her? Who's she gonna tell? I can't imagine she isn't bugging you to know," Butch said.

"Course she is. I wanted to do it this way."

Hoyt stared at his cards. "Shoulda kept the vows as they were, *man* and wife. Would've been truer. Partnership? Mighty strange definition." He said "partnership" as if it were a curse word.

He hadn't made a comment earlier when they'd talked about the vows, so why now? Tony counted to five before he answered. "That's not fair. I wanted it to be a surprise for her. My gift to her."

"May look like that. Fold." He tossed down his cards.

All the attention shifted to Hoyt.

"What do you think it is?" Tony asked.

"You bein' boss. You're old-school. It's showin'."

"You figure I got that from you?" Tony asked.

"Hard to go against your upbringing. Pretty ingrained."

"I'm nothing like you." *Nothing.* Tony had made sure of that.

The room got quiet.

"You're a rancher," Hoyt pointed out.

"I'm also a poker player and a stock market investor." He kept his substantial investments, seeded in the beginning with his poker winnings, separate from the ranch funds, which he needed to be self-sustaining. "You ever take risks like that? No. You play it safe. That's a big difference between us."

"True. I never had extra to play with. Provided for my family just fine, though."

"We got by, sure. But 'provide'? Depends on how you look at that word."

"How do *you* look at it?"

Cal, Grady and Butch quietly left the room, leaving father and son alone.

"Son? I'm waitin'."

Tony didn't want to have this discussion—this argument. It'd been brewing too long. Could get too emotional. He started picking up the poker chips and putting them in the trays. "Not now, Dad."

"You've been holdin' back for years. No better time than now. You're startin' a new life. I like your girl, by the way. Got spunk."

Of all the things he could have said, it was the worst—a reminder of the fact the marriage would end almost before it began.

"I'm glad I finally did something you approve of," Tony said. Too bad it wouldn't last. "Took me long enough."

"What the hell does that mean?"

That he even had to ask staggered Tony. Every repressed emotion, every old hurt, came tumbling out. "All my life I've been trying to prove myself to you. I brought home trophies, and you said nothing. I won championships, and you stood there while everyone else congratulated me, not saying a word."

Tony shoved the tray of chips. It fell off the table, scattering them on the floor. "I got inducted into the hall of fame, and you were there, watching the whole ceremony, then…nothing. Not a word, just a handshake, like I was someone you hardly knew." He tunneled his fingers through his hair. "I got myself engaged to Maggie McShane. No comment. All that success, and…nothing. You've never believed in me, accepted me."

The eye-opening self-revelation had Tony jerking back

from its impact. He hadn't been trying to prove his *success* all these years. No, he'd wanted to be *accepted,* just as he was, as a man who was different from Cal and Grady, different from his father. Anthony Young, an individual. A son loved only for himself, his existence, nothing more.

"You always held yourself apart," Hoyt said. "But I did accept you."

"I know better. I heard you say it yourself. You never wanted me. Never thought I'd make anything of myself."

The lines on his father's face trenched deeper. "You better explain that."

Tony walked away from him as the memories filled his head again, memories he blocked most of the time. "I was twelve."

"I remember that year. You went from bein' a gabber to hardly talkin' at all."

"After I learned the truth."

"About what?"

"I came upon you and Mom, having a discussion about me."

"What'd you hear?"

"You were telling her you should've stopped at three kids, like you'd planned all along."

"Hell, son, every parent says that when their kid is being ornery. Don't mean nothing by it. You're every bit as important as the others."

"You said I always had my head in the clouds, thinking only about rodeoing."

"Well, that was a fact you can't dispute. Was all you talked about. Always out practicing, disregarding your schoolwork, hardly coming in to eat unless we threatened you. So? That's a crime, too, telling the truth?"

And then the worst of what he'd overheard. "You told Mom I'd never make it in rodeo."

Hoyt stared at him for the longest time, then he put both hands on Tony's shoulders. "That was a turnin' point for me, too, son. That discussion with your mom. I knew the rodeo world. On talent alone, you were bound to succeed. But I was talkin' about survivin' it."

With Hoyt's hands on his shoulders, Tony had no choice but to focus on his father's face. "What do you mean?"

"Well, first there was the finances. I knew how much it cost to launch a rodeo career. Even back in those days, it took a pile of dough just to get up and running."

"Right. So?"

"Your mom and I couldn't afford to help you."

"I got sponsors. I slept on the ground. Ate out of cans."

"And how much were your winnings that first year?"

Tony's mouth twisted. "About three grand."

Hoyt nodded. "And then the mental survival. You were a dreamer, son. A hard worker, but a dreamer. I did what I could so that you would survive in that world, a hard one, sometimes a vicious one."

"By bein' harder on me than you were on Cal or Grady?"

"Was I? Maybe so. I didn't coddle you. Couldn't. You wouldn't've survived the circuit if I had. By the time you left home, you were tough. I made sure of it."

"And angry."

"Sometimes that's what a man needs."

Tony tried to sort through the revelations. "You believed I could be a winner?"

"No doubt about it—if it was based on skill alone. You were hell-bent on suffering all kinds of abuse, even just practicin'. Nothin' I could've said to you would've changed your mind. You were born to it. And, son? I love all you kids the same. You'll see. When you're a father, you'll see."

When he was a father…

Hoyt's cell phone rang. He looked at the screen, raised his brows as he answered. "Yeah, he's here with me," Hoyt said. "What? Right. I'll tell him." He closed the phone and slid it into his shirt pocket.

"That was Dino. Seems you've got a bit of a problem, son." Tony went rigid. "Maggie?"

"She's fine, I guess. But she's got a visitor. One Scott Gibson. She—"

But Tony was out of the room before Hoyt finished.

Chapter Seventeen

"He's already out in the hallway," Dino said to Maggie.

"You brought Scott Gibson up here? To my suite? Without asking me? How could you do that?"

"Because you have to talk to him sometime, and I didn't want a ruckus in the lobby. Seemed easier this way."

"On my wedding day?"

"Why not? You're just killing time at the moment."

Maggie's hair and makeup were done. She'd just sent everyone away, wanting a little time alone before her stylist and Leesa came back to help her dress.

"Tell him I'll give him five minutes," she said. "And don't tell Tony."

Then she sat down and waited for the man who'd started the whole thing, the man she should thank with all her heart...

He'd kept his hair blond and spiked with gel. It suited him, Maggie thought objectively as he came toward her.

When they'd met, he'd had dark hair, styled like a business-man. *That* Scott would've suited her—or the Maggie she'd been at the time, not the woman she'd become. This ultra-contemporary man didn't suit her at all.

She looked at her watch. "Four minutes and fifty seconds," she said.

He grinned.

"Four minutes and forty…"

"Okay, okay." He moved closer, until they almost touched.

Maggie stood her ground, refusing to let him get to her.

"I know you don't love him," Scott said.

She raised her brows dramatically high. "Really? And you would know that *how?*"

"I have my ways."

She laughed and stepped away from him. Dino and Leesa would've been the only ones who could've been close enough to make any kind of judgment about such things, and they would never talk. He was grasping at straws. She wondered why. "If you paid money for that bit of information, you got counterfeit data."

His smile faltered a little.

"So, how's Gennifer?" Maggie asked. "Oh, no, I'm sorry. I heard she's moved on to Morgan Kristoff. Isn't that just a shame. Of course, since you pretended to the press that she'd just been a rebound gone wrong, you're still the good guy to the world."

"Go ahead, have your fun. I can take it. You haven't thrown me out, so I figure you're still carrying a flame. It's not too late to go back to the original plan, you know."

"You're such a kidder." She tapped her watch. "So, why are you really here, Scott?"

"I told you. I want you back. I don't know what was

wrong with me, why I gave you up, but my head's on straight now."

"Actually you didn't say you wanted me back. And for the record? You don't want me back. You're using this opportunity as a publicity stunt. Show up on my wedding day, act like you want me back and keep your name in the rags, the poor, sad, besotted, dumped fiancé. I know how it all works."

"A little publicity never hurt anyone, but that's not why I'm here." He moved closer.

The door opened. Tony came through, his expression hard, his movements stiff but not faltering for a second.

"I thought the groom wasn't supposed to see the bride until the ceremony," Scott said, looking a little less sure of himself as he watched Tony cross the room and stand next to Maggie. Tony slid an arm around her waist. He was entirely controlled, but she figured he was pretty angry. Whether he was angry at her or Scott, she didn't know.

"Hi," she said, trying to convey everything she felt in that one word. *I love you. Please don't make a scene.*

"You doin' okay, Margaret?"

Margaret. Was it for show or for real?

"I'm fine, thank you."

He faced Scott then. "Where I come from, men don't infringe on another man's territory."

Maggie should have been offended by the chauvinism, but she was encouraged that she was his territory, so she kept quiet. Obviously he hadn't yet figured out Scott was just trying to get some attention for himself.

"I happened to be in town," Scott said. "I'm only paying a visit to an old friend." He didn't look at all confident anymore, probably because Tony was being quiet and calm. It was throwing Scott off. Her, too, for that matter.

"Do you call that Gennifer Bodine an old friend, too?" Tony asked. "That relationship lasted about as long as a knee jerk, didn't it? Must be humiliating, losing all your women so fast."

His chin went up. "I don't know what Maggie told you, but I didn't lose her. I gave her up. I'm pretty sure she wants me back."

"I know exactly what happened," Tony said. "She shared the truth with me. And as for wanting you back, let's just ask her." He met her gaze. "You want to change grooms again?"

"No."

"*No*," he said, even duplicating the succinct tone. "The lady says no. You can be on your way now. And if you get so much as one finger in a photograph that appears from our wedding, I'll make sure you live to regret it."

"Tough guy."

"I take care of my own."

The change in atmosphere happened in an instant. Neither of them had thrown down a gauntlet, but they might as well have. She sensed that one more insult from Scott would have Tony all over him.

"Scott, you can leave now," Maggie said, putting a hand on Tony's chest, as if that would stop him from charging.

"Stay out of it, Margaret."

When had she lost control of her life?

"I'm going," Scott said, backing up, his hands up in surrender mode.

"He's only after publicity," she said to Tony.

"It's a two-for-one deal," Scott said. "I get publicity and another chance with her. I wish I hadn't broken things off with her. What's wrong with telling the world?"

"Where I come from," Tony said, "men handle problems between them. They don't involve the world."

"I'm only interested in Maggie's well-being. I'm not sure you're the right man for her." Scott looked at her. "You can still marry me. You don't have to be stuck with the choice you made to save face."

Her response was to move to the door, open it and speak to Dino. "Take Mr. Gibson out of the hotel and see that he's put in a cab, please?"

Dino looked to Tony. She caught him nodding, a tiny movement. When had Dino started needing Tony to confirm an order she gave? It ticked her off but good.

"My pleasure," Dino said. "Mr. Gibson?"

Scott stopped when he reached her side. "I'm seeing issues between you two. You ever need a friend…"

Dino shut the door before he could finish, leaving the bride and groom alone.

"Well, that was…interesting," she said, using as vague a word as she could come up with.

"You didn't discourage him much," Tony said.

"He's not a bad guy, you know. Egotistical and career-driven, but I think he was sincere, in his own self-absorbed way. I like to think I'm not *that* bad a judge of character."

"He gave you an out, Margaret. If you want to take him up on it, tell me now, before Dino puts him in the cab."

Margaret. Why was it she got such hope from him calling her that? Because it seemed more natural? More real? Or was he just conditioned to it?

She'd been moving slowly toward him and now was close enough to touch. She didn't. "I don't want him back."

"That's not an answer. My question was, do you want out?

Because I don't want you out of obligation or a deal made. I thought I did. Even last night, I thought that. Not anymore."

"Same goes for me."

They both went silent. Who talks first? she wondered. And will it be the truth or a guess about what the other one was feeling?

It needed to be her, she decided. Because he wouldn't say it first…

"I love you, Margaret."

Her mouth went dry. "You do?"

Tony nodded his head ruefully. "I think I fell in love with you on the dance floor, because I never would've agreed to your crazy plan if I hadn't wanted you to be mine forever, period. If you marry me tonight, it's for life, not as a way of saving face or fulfilling a PR promise or keeping a deal. There won't be any divorce, not in a couple of weeks or months or decades, even. You'll be stuck with me for life."

Her heart pounded so loud she could barely hear him, but his eyes had gone all tender, just like when Richard had looked at Jenny. Wishes did come true, after all.

"I love you, too, cowboy. That's what I was trying to tell you yesterday. I didn't want to marry you unless you knew I never wanted it to end."

He took her hands in his. "That's probably not somethin' you should've given up on telling me. You should've shouted it at me, made me listen, don't you think?"

"You cut me off. You walked away. And I let you so I could justify going through with the marriage, knowing I wouldn't end it. I figured if I had more time, I could get you to love me. Did you just now realize you loved me? Are you sure it's not just possessiveness or something?"

"I just now let it sink into my thick head, but I've been feeling it for a while without letting it shout out. Maybe because everything seemed to be running so smoothly between us, I couldn't believe it was real, but a game we were playing."

"No games. Ever."

He bent low, pressed his lips to hers. "No secrets, then. Ever. Okay?"

Her eyes burned, her heart swelled. "I'll even give up acting. I want to be a good ranch wife. I—"

He laughed. The sound was so beautiful, she could only smile.

"Darlin', you can't give up acting. You want to take it easier, slower? Fine. But don't toss away the gift you have. We'll work things out."

"Even after the babies come?"

He nodded, his gaze going even more tender. "We're a team now. We'll figure it out together."

Maggie threw her arms around him and held on tight. "What do you say we get married? I'm ready for a honeymoon. How about you?"

"Definitely."

"When are you going to tell me where we're going?"

"On a plane."

"See? I told you before you like to keep me guessing."

"Not about the important things. Like how much I love you."

"That suits me fine, cowboy. Just fine."

* * * * *

Chapter 1

October
New York City

Nicole Masters was sitting cross-legged on her sofa while a cold autumn rain peppered the windows of her fourth-floor apartment. She was poking at the ice cream in her bowl and trying not to be in a mood.

Six weeks ago, a simple trip to her neighborhood pharmacy had turned into a nightmare. She'd walked into the middle of a robbery. She never even saw the man who shot her in the head and left her for dead. She'd survived, but some of her senses had not. She was dealing with short-term memory loss and a tendency to stagger. Even though she'd been told the problems were most likely temporary, she waged a daily battle with depression.

Her parents had been killed in a car wreck when she was twenty-one. And except for a few friends—and most recently her boyfriend, Dominic Tucci, who lived in the apartment right above hers, she was alone. Her doctor kept reminding her that she should be grateful to be alive, and on one level she knew he was right. But he wasn't living in her shoes.

If she'd been anywhere else but at that pharmacy when the robbery happened, she wouldn't have died twice on the way to the hospital. Instead of being grateful that she'd survived, she couldn't stop thinking of what she'd lost.

But that wasn't the end of her troubles. On top of everything else, something strange was happening inside her head. She'd begun to hear odd things: sounds, not voices—at least, she didn't think it was voices. It was more like the distant noise of rapids—a rush of wind and water inside her head that, when it came, blocked out everything around her. It didn't happen often, but when it did, it was frightening, and it was driving her crazy.

The blank moments, which is what she called them, even had a rhythm. First there came that sound, then a cold sweat, then panic with no reason. Part of her feared it was the beginning of an emotional breakdown. And part of her feared it wasn't—that it was going to turn out to be a permanent souvenir of her resurrection.

Frustrated with herself and the situation as it stood, she upped the sound on the TV remote. But instead of *Wheel of Fortune,* an announcer broke in with a special bulletin.

"This just in. Police are on the scene of a kidnapping that occurred only hours ago at The Dakota. Molly Dane, the six-year-old daughter of one of Hollywood's blockbuster stars, Lyla Dane, was taken by force from the family apartment. At this time they have yet to receive a ransom demand. The house-keeper was seriously injured during the abduction, and is, at the present time, in surgery. Police are hoping to be able to talk to her once she regains con-sciousness. In the meantime, we are going now to a press conference with Lyla Dane."

Horrified, Nicole stilled as the cameras went live to where the actress was speaking before a bank of micro-phones. The shock and terror in Lyla Dane's voice were physically painful to watch. But even though Nicole kept upping the volume, the sound continued to fade.

Just when she was beginning to think something was wrong with her set, the broadcast suddenly switched from the Dane press conference to what appeared to be footage of the kidnapping, beginning with footage from inside the apartment.

When the front door suddenly flew back against the wall and four men rushed in, Nicole gasped. Horrified, she quickly realized that this must have been caught on a security camera inside the Dane apartment.

As Nicole continued to watch, a small Asian woman, who she guessed was the maid, rushed forward in an effort to keep them out. When one of the men hit her in the face with his gun, Nicole moaned. The violence was too remi-niscent of what she'd lived through. Sick to her stomach, she fisted her hands against her belly, wishing it was over, but unable to tear her gaze away.

When the maid dropped to the carpet, the same man followed with a vicious kick to the little woman's midsec-tion that lifted her off the floor.

"Oh, my God," Nicole said. When blood began to pool beneath the maid's head, she started to cry.

As the tape played on, the four men split up in different directions. The camera caught one running down a long marble hallway, then disappearing into a room. Moments later he reappeared, carrying a little girl, who Nicole assumed was Molly Dane. The child was wearing a pair of red pants and a white turtleneck sweater, and her hair was partially blocking her abductor's face as he carried her down the hall. She was kicking and screaming in his arms, and when he slapped her, it elicited an agonized scream that brought the other three running. Nicole watched in horror as one of them ran up and put his hand over Molly's face. Seconds later, she went limp.

One moment they were in the foyer, then they were gone.

Nicole jumped to her feet, then staggered drunkenly. The bowl of ice cream she'd absentmindedly placed in her lap shattered at her feet, splattering glass and melting ice cream everywhere.

The picture on the screen abruptly switched from the kidnapping to what Nicole assumed was a rerun of Lyla Dane's plea for her daughter's safe return, but she was numb.

Before she could think what to do next, the doorbell rang. Startled by the unexpected sound, she shakily swiped at the tears and took a step forward. She didn't feel the glass shards piercing her feet until she took the second step. At that point, sharp pains shot through her foot. She gasped, then looked down in confusion. Her legs looked as if she'd been running through mud, and she was standing in broken glass and ice cream, while a thin ribbon of blood seeped out from beneath her toes.

"Oh, no," Nicole mumbled, then stifled a second moan of pain.

The doorbell rang again. She shivered, then clutched her head in confusion.

"Just a minute!" she yelled, then tried to sidestep the rest of the debris as she hobbled to the door.

When she looked through the peephole in the door, she didn't know whether to be relieved or regretful.

It was Dominic, and as usual, she was a mess.

Nicole smiled a little self-consciously as she opened the door to let him in. "I just don't know what's happening to me. I think I'm losing my mind."

"Hey, don't talk about my woman like that."

Nicole rode the surge of delight his words brought. "So I'm still your woman?"

Dominic lowered his head.

Their lips met.

The kiss proceeded.

Slowly.

Thoroughly.

* * * * *

Be sure to look for the AFTERSHOCK *anthology next month, as well as other exciting paranormal stories from Silhouette Nocturne.*
Available in October wherever books are sold.

nocturne™

NEW YORK TIMES BESTSELLING AUTHOR

SHARON SALA

JANIS REAMES HUDSON
DEBRA COWAN

———

AFTERSHOCK

Three women are brought to the brink of death...
only to discover the aftershock of their trauma has
left them with unexpected and unwelcome gifts of
paranormal powers. Now each woman must learn to
accept her newfound abilities while fighting for life,
love and second chances....

Available October wherever books are sold.

SPECIAL EDITION™

BRAVO FAMILY TIES

Tanner Bravo and Crystal Cerise had it bad
for each other, though they couldn't be more
different. Tanner was the type to settle down;
free-spirited Crystal wouldn't hear of it.
Now that Crystal was pregnant, would
Tanner have his way after all?

Look for

HAVING
TANNER BRAVO'S
BABY

by *USA TODAY* bestselling author
CHRISTINE RIMMER

Available in October wherever books are sold.

REQUEST YOUR FREE BOOKS!

2 FREE NOVELS PLUS 2 FREE GIFTS!

SPECIAL EDITION®

Life, Love and Family!

YES! Please send me 2 FREE Silhouette Special Edition® novels and my 2 FREE gifts (gifts are worth about $10). After receiving them, if I don't wish to receive any more books, I can return the shipping statement marked "cancel." If I don't cancel, I will receive 6 brand-new novels every month and be billed just $4.24 per book in the U.S. or $4.99 per book in Canada, plus 25¢ shipping and handling per book and applicable taxes, if any*. That's a savings of at least 15% off the cover price! I understand that accepting the 2 free books and gifts places me under no obligation to buy anything. I can always return a shipment and cancel at any time. Even if I never buy another book from Silhouette, the two free books and gifts are mine to keep forever.

235 SDN EEYU   335 SDN EEY6

Name	(PLEASE PRINT)

Address	Apt. #

City	State/Prov.	Zip/Postal Code

Signature (if under 18, a parent or guardian must sign)

Mail to the **Silhouette Reader Service:**
IN U.S.A.: P.O. Box 1867, Buffalo, NY 14240-1867
IN CANADA: P.O. Box 609, Fort Erie, Ontario L2A 5X3

Not valid to current subscribers of Silhouette Special Edition books.

Want to try two free books from another line?
Call 1-800-873-8635 or visit www.morefreebooks.com.

* Terms and prices subject to change without notice. N.Y. residents add applicable sales tax. Canadian residents will be charged applicable provincial taxes and GST. Offer not valid in Quebec. This offer is limited to one order per household. All orders subject to approval. Credit or debit balances in a customer's account(s) may be offset by any other outstanding balance owed by or to the customer. Please allow 4 to 6 weeks for delivery. Offer available while quantities last.

Your Privacy: Silhouette is committed to protecting your privacy. Our Privacy Policy is available online at www.eHarlequin.com or upon request from the Reader Service. From time to time we make our lists of customers available to reputable third parties who may have a product or service of interest to you. If you would prefer we not share your name and address, please check here. ☐

SSE08R

COMING NEXT MONTH

SPECIAL EDITION

#1927 HAVING TANNER BRAVO'S BABY—Christine Rimmer
Bravo Family Ties

Tanner Bravo and Crystal Cerise had it bad for each other, though they couldn't be more different. Tanner was the type to settle down; free-spirited Crystal wouldn't hear of it. Now that Crystal was pregnant, would Tanner have his way after all?

#1928 FAMILY IN PROGRESS—Brenda Harlen
Back in Business

Restoring classic cars was widowed dad Steven Warren's stock in trade. And when magazine photographer Samara Kenzo showed up to snap his masterpieces, her focus was squarely on the handsome mechanic. But the closer they got, the more Steven's preteen daughter objected to this interloper....

#1929 HOMETOWN SWEETHEART—Victoria Pade
Northbridge Nuptials

When Wyatt Grayson's elderly grandmother showed up, disoriented and raving, in her hometown, it was social worker Neily Pratt to the rescue. And while her job was to determine if Wyatt was a fit guardian for his grandmother, Neily knew right away that she'd appoint him guardian of her own heart any day!

#1930 THE SINGLE DAD'S VIRGIN WIFE—Susan Crosby
Wives for Hire

Tricia McBride was in the mood for adventure, and that's just what she got when she agreed to homeschool Noah Falcon's two sets of twins. As she warmed to the charms of this single dad, Tricia realized that what started out strictly business was turning into pure pleasure....

#1931 ACCIDENTAL PRINCESS—Nancy Robards Thompson

Most little girls dream of being a princess—single mom Sophie Baldwin's world turned upside down when she found out she was one! As this social-worker-turned-sovereign rightfully claimed the throne of St. Michel, little did she know she was claiming the heart of St. Michel's Minister of Security, Philippe Lejardin, in the process.

#1932 FALLING FOR THE LONE WOLF—Crystal Green
The Suds Club

Her friends at the Suds Club Laundromat noticed that something was up with Jenny Hunter—especially Web consultant Liam McCree, who had designs on the businesswoman. Would serial-dating Jenny end up with this secret admirer? Or would a looming health crisis stand in their way? It would all come out in the wash....

SSECNM0908